# Silent Farm

### Written by,
### Jack Hemphill

Published by
Willow Oak Publishing

Library of Congress Control Number: 2018905711
ISBN: 978-0-9899516-3-0
Printed in the United States of America

Cover image: painted by Jack Hemphill
Graphic design: Ashley Bird, Birdhill Design

# INTRODUCTION

After the Second World War, an old building used as a bookstore sat directly across Franklin Street from the University of North Carolina Campus. For years, the old store had been a gathering place for students to discuss and debate ideas. One of the most hotly debated topics was communism, which was growing rapidly across parts of Europe but was barely understood by most Americans.

Communism was vigorously opposed by the University and by most of its students; however, at the end of the decade, the Communist Party headquarters for North and South Carolina, Virginia, Tennessee, and part of Mississippi was in Chapel Hill.

Information gathered for this novel from the writings of FBI Agents, communist leaders, and historical documents were used to illustrate the events, characters, and ideals that grew out of that pivotal period in American History between 1946 and 1956.

The following forty-two chapters were written through the eyes of communists and through the eyes of people whose lives were severely altered by communism.

Communism is an ideology, and, like any ideology, its substance and movement is found growing in the human mind. Literature that explores this journey frequently depends on the use of metaphors to help visualize some of its abstract ideas. Welcome to the Silent Farm.

# CHAPTER ONE

## LEM
### MAY 1946

I grew out of black soil and red clay, doodlebugs, sweet gum balls, arrowheads, summer thunder, firecrackers smuggled from South Carolina, and the white down of ducklings. I smelled like cracked corn and wet straw. I loved forest sounds before sunrise. I sweated away every ounce of energy during the day and slept quiet as a dead stump at night.

Except for crops used for feed, we raised nothing but ducks on our farm, beautiful white Peking ducks. When I was a boy, I was never allowed to think of our white feathered flock as anything but a crop, like corn or turnips, but my sister, Trish, and I knew each duck and selected our favorites for laying and breeding. Over the years, we watched thousands of them hatch and grow. The ducks were never afraid of anything as long as we were with them, even when I loaded them in small cages on the back of my pickup and hauled them away to market or turned them over to be slaughtered by Quincy, our only farmhand. Our house was a good quarter mile from the nearest neighbor. We had fifty acres wedged into a sharp bend in the Haw River, about ten miles south of Chapel

Hill.

I remember a day in the summer of 1946. Trish had something big to tell me. I knew it because all morning she looked as if she was holding her breath, waiting for the right time. Trish thought too much. Maybe that was her only fault. She brooded over every decision, so I knew not to ask what was on her mind. She would tell me when she was ready. I had no idea that what was stewing inside her would eventually change both our lives.

I finished letting the adult ducks out of their pens and watched them being led by the lead drake into the water. The flock moved effortlessly and silently around the pond like a cloud in soft wind. They swam for over an hour, but when the leader saw me carrying the feed bags to the pens, he turned toward me, and, in a single motion, all the others paddled behind him to the bank and waddled to their feeding areas. Like soldiers dressed in white, they lined along the troughs while I poured grain from burlap bags. They were fed twice a day. I loved to watch their little heads, all six hundred of them, eagerly bobbing up and down as if the grain would run out any minute. But to make sure they were plump for market, they were fed as much as they would eat.

After feeding the ducks, I looked for Trish. No sign of her. She didn't answer when I called her name. I left the feeding area, closed the gate behind me, then walked past the brooding pens. That's where Trish took special care of the little ones. The first thing every duck saw as he pecked his way out of the shell was Trish's face watching them come into the world, and the first thing they felt was her hands holding them and cleaning them. For the entire time they lived on the farm, they saw her as their only mother. I called her name again. Still, no answer.

We always kept the young ducklings in the brooding area until they were five weeks old. That was their most vulnerable stage. One duckling died about every two weeks. Before Trish was old enough to work the incubation and brooding pen area, Quincy threw the little dead duckling bodies into the compost, fifty yards away from the house. But Trish could never do that any more than she could watch the adult ducks being slaughtered. There is a flat area behind the pump house that Trish turned into a duck graveyard. She carefully dug each grave twelve inches apart. From the creek, she gathered hand-sized rocks and placed one on each grave. By then, there were hundreds of graves all lined up in neat columns and rows. I had a hard time understanding why she did it. To me it was silly, but it didn't matter, I never claimed to understand her.

I leaned against the stone wall on the shady side of the pump house and watched her carefully dig the little hole. Thoughtfully she placed the body in the grave. After packing the earth and securing the stone, she sat silently for a full minute. I didn't know if she was silently talking to the dead duckling or saying a prayer for it.

She didn't notice me until she had walked halfway back to the pump house.

"Lem, I didn't see you!" she said, startled.

"Didn't want to disturb you *Little Broody*." That's what I called Trish ever since she was a little girl. *Broody* is the name for a duck with mothering instincts.

"Lost another one," she said.

"It's okay. Not your fault."

She looked down as she walked past me.

"Sorry 'bout that thing at your school today," I said softly.

Without answering, she sat on the hill overlooking the smaller pond, which was used entirely for young ducklings. We needed two ponds to separate the little ones from the full-grown ducks and drakes in the larger pond. I sat beside her on the hill and leaned back on my elbows against the soft grass.

Trish sat slightly in front of me, so I was able to watch her and the little flock below us at the same time. She was perched in her usual position with legs crossed at the ankles, hands folded in her lap, head held high above her perfectly straight back. She could sit comfortably like that for hours, which fascinated me because if I tried, I couldn't sit that way for ten minutes without squirming into a new position. Her dark brown hair was short and curly but long enough to tie into a little ponytail. She still had the face of a young girl with brown freckles dappled across her round cheeks and nose. Her face always contained a hidden smile. That peaceful picture of her sitting on the hill watching the little ducks is the strongest memory of her I ever had, and I still see it in my mind every day. Her gaze was so fixed on the ducks that I'm sure she forgot all about me for a while.

After waiting another fifteen minutes, I said again, "I really am sorry about upsettin' your friend today."

She turned her head toward me and asked, "Why don't you like him?"

"No reason other than he looks hungry, and stares at you like you're a piece of pie, and half the school thinks he's nothing' but a *hayseed*…I can't imagine what you see in him."

6

"He seems nice and always wants to walk me home," she replied.

"And *that's* what ya see in him?"

"Yes."

"Nothin' else?"

"No! Why do I need something else?"

"Oh Broody...I understand you never want to hurt anyone's feelin's and all that, but there are some people you jus' can't trust."

"I *know* that Lem; I'm not a child! I'll be eighteen next month."

"That's my point. They're not lookin' at you now like you're still a *child*."

"What's wrong with that?" she said shaking her head slightly and shifting a few inches away. After regaining her position, with her hands in her lap, she said, "You *gotta* leave me alone."

"Okay, I will."

"Then stop walking me home from school every day. What do you think my friends think of that?"

"I don't care what they think."

"I know you don't, but *I* care...And I'm embarrassed."

"*I* embarrass you?"

"It's your hovering over me all the time. Most boys won't even look at me when you're around."

"Why?"

"You know why."

"No. Tell me."

"You know they're *afraid* of you."

"Why?"

"Because you're a six-foot-eight *monster*. *Freak*! As far as I know, you're the tallest guy in all North Carolina.

7

Most of the boys won't get close to me, because I'm your sister."

"*Good!*"

"No Lem, *not good.*"

We stopped talking for a while and watched the flock's pageant moving silently, like a mindless yellow-white wreath circling a large dark hole. The bigger, faster ducks waggled their way to the outside edge of the revolving ring surrounding the smaller ones who undoubtedly felt protected from predators by the shroud of larger ducks.

"Promise me you won't walk me home tomorrow."

"Okay Broody, I promise. I won't walk you home for the rest of the school year — if that's what you want."

"That's what I want." Neither of us mentioned there was only one week left before she graduated from Chatham County High School.

"One more thing," she said, "You have to stop calling me Broody."

After another long gaze at the flock, she rolled to her knees, faced me, and said with a totally new voice, "Now I've got good news. Been waiting to stop being mad at you, so I can tell you all about it."

"Well, to me, the good news is you stopped bein' mad, but what did you want to tell me?"

"I got the job!"

"The one at the bookstore?"

"Yes!"

"You are sure this is what you wanta do?"

"It seems like it would be really exciting. I'm going to drive to Chapel Hill on Saturday and check it out."

"When do you start?"

"Not until the end of the summer. Got plenty of time."

"You're gonna need the car?"

"Well, most of the time, but just to get to work and back. If you need it, can you drop me off in the morning and pick me up in the afternoon?"

"Exactly where in Chapel Hill is this store?"

"Right in the middle, on Franklin Street."

"Okay, 'bout a fifteen-minute drive?"

"Yes."

"We'll work it out. So, what's this place called?"

"*Community Bookstore.*"

"How did you get the job?"

"My English teacher, Miss. Ward, worked there years ago when she was a student, and she knows the owner of the store. She said I'm just the kind of person they're looking for, so she recommended me."

"That's great!" I loved to see Trish so happy, and I had to pretend to be happy too. "Have you told Mom?"

"Yes."

"Did she understand?"

"I don't know, don't think so, but she smiled anyway."

Six years separated our ages, but after Dad died, it seemed like more than that. We were closer to each other than we ever were to our parents. Whenever Trish fell down, I was always the one who put the Band-Aids on her knees. I'm the only one who drank her sour lemonade, watched her on the playground, rode her on my bike in the rain, buried her dog when he died, and walked her home from school every single day.

Mom was never the same after Dad died, and when Trish was old enough, she took care of Mom every day and helped with the farm chores.

Two months before Trish started working in Chapel

Hill, our aunt and uncle offered to keep Mom at their house near Pittsboro. Trish cried when our cousins took Mom away, but we knew she needed a grown woman to take care of her, and soon Trish would be going to work. Mother only lived another month.

I couldn't imagine Trish not working on the farm — not that I was concerned about running it by myself. I had Quincy to help me, and he was stronger than three men. I just couldn't picture her anywhere else. She never traveled, never had a job outside the farm, and judging from her reactions to some of the books she read, movies she watched, and even some of the silly cartoons she saw at the picture show, she was extremely emotional. But maybe all girls her age are emotional. I had no way of knowing.

# CHAPTER TWO

## TRISH
### AUGUST 1946

I graduated from high school that year, and my mind was filled with wonderful, imaginary things that could be in store for me at my new job in Chapel Hill.

My earliest memories go back to summers on the farm. I remember cooling my bare feet in the pond, eating butter sandwiches sprinkled with sugar, drinking endless cups of lemonade, and making long clover necklaces that covered my chest with tiny white flowers. Even though Lem was six years older than me, he knew what I loved and never tired of talking about the little girl world in my imagination. I can remember when I was three, and Lem was pushing nine. Even then, he was so tall I thought of him as a giant, like the one in the *Jack and the Beanstalk* story Mamma read to me at night. That's when I started calling Lem, *Blunderbore,* after that great giant in the Beanstalk story. Lem was always nice to me, but as far back as I can remember, everybody I knew was afraid of him — not because of his disposition but because of his sheer size.

The most memorable book Mom read to me was Charlotte's Web. I was afraid of spiders, until she read that book and, only a few weeks after the first time she read it, I found a large, beautiful, yellow spider on her web under the eaves of the feed storage shed. *My own Charlotte*, I thought, enjoying life and trapping insects. Almost daily, I ran down the hill to see what she was doing. She continually moved from corner to corner of her web, patching up her house, anchoring the web, and then sitting perfectly still, waiting for her next victim. After a while, a small gray fuzzy pouch appeared in the web.

One cool morning at the end of summer, a mist hung over the farm. By 9:00 o'clock, rays of sunshine broke through an opening in the clouds, and shot clear, bright beams of light around the yard. One sunbeam landed square on top of the feed shed. I ran down to the shed to see my little friend. She was gone, but her fuzzy gray bag had opened, letting out armies of tiny yellow baby spiders moving in all directions. The web shimmered and shined in the light, while the spider children crawled over countless small drops of mist reflecting the sun and making the web look like a bright star attached between the shed and the fence. Slowly the little armies left the web to find a thousand places to weave their own webs, trap insects, grow, and produce their own little spider babies. I was told that ducks ate spiders, but, thankfully, I didn't see any being eaten that day. For years after that, I found yellow spiders hiding on webs in the corners of the pens, in the fields, on the back of the house, on fence posts, and eventually beyond the house. They all started out so small, silent, and secret, that I believe if I had never found my little Charlotte, I probably would not have ever noticed the yellow creatures spreading around the farm.

I always felt safe with Lem, my *Blunderbore*, and he let me laugh, and scream, and be as silly as I wanted. The sillier I was, the more he loved it.

I don't remember Daddy. He died when I was two. Mamma spent most of her days in the kitchen, and she loved reading to me. I guess I was around ten before I realized that she never went out of the house. It just seemed so natural for her to always be inside doing what she wanted to do. Her sister helped with the groceries until Lem was twelve and could walk to the store three to four times a week by himself. I know it made him feel grown-up. By then, he was as big as any high school student. He wanted to be outside all the time and was afraid of nothing. He did everything for me, Mom, and the farm. Just the three of us lived together in our little farmhouse surrounded by six hundred ducks.

•••

I was eighteen, and had never been more than forty miles from home. I never thought about leaving it until my English teacher got me the bookstore job. Saturday morning was always the best day to drive into Chapel Hill — very little traffic. It usually took about fifteen minutes to make the trip, but I drove slowly just to keep my excitement down. I passed the store and parked a block and a half further up the street. That way I could look at the store from a distance and walk down the sidewalk to the building like I was just another customer, maybe a UNC student. The front of the store was quite simple. It had an old brick face with a wood door right in the center. The door was covered by a large awning. On either side of the door were two large windows used for displaying books.

I cupped my hands over my eyes and peeped into the left window and saw a young woman standing behind a counter. Her arms were crossed as she watched something going on in the store.

The front of the building looked straight across Franklin Street into the center of the UNC campus. I stood there five full minutes gazing at the campus and gathering my courage before going inside. The woman behind the counter glanced at me for only a brief moment and then returned her attention to voices in the back of the room. At first, I thought they were angry voices until the whole crowd broke out in a hearty laugh then melted back into fierce debate. Pretending to be looking for a book, I walked between two freestanding bookshelves until I could see into the back corner of the room. A group of about eight people, mostly boys, were sitting in a circle on wood chairs or cushioned seats. A few sat on the floor. Whatever they were debating was clearly important to each of them, and no one held back his opinions. I assumed they were mostly UNC students, and a few may have been professors or something like that.

I walked to the side of their circle and listened. They all spoke with passion and conviction about topics I never thought of. They talked about things going on in other parts of the country, like New York, and Washington, and Atlanta. One man discussed something going on in Russia, and another man quoted a line in a foreign language. I think it was French. I heard the terms *collectivism* and *fascism* mentioned several times. The loudest parts of the discussion came, when they talked about the plight of the poor in the country, and about what they called the *Negro Nation*, a term I had never heard before. Although I understood most of the words and generally knew what they were talking about, I couldn't understand any of the subtle details being debated. Most of the time I couldn't even tell if they were agreeing or disagreeing.

They didn't notice me at all. I felt like a little girl, in bare feet, with white clover necklaces dangling around my neck. I turned, tiptoed away, and walked along the back of the store, which was covered with bookshelves eight feet high and stuffed with old books.

I walked around the room one more time and nodded at the woman behind the counter, who returned a nod. Halfway to my car, I looked back at the store. From that distance, it looked like a simple small-town bookstore, and I felt a little better, but if my purpose that day was to quiet my fears about working there, I failed.

Jack Hemphill

# CHAPTER THREE

## WILL
## SEPTEMBER 1946

I started graduate studies at Chapel Hill in August 1946. I finally knew what I was doing with my life. All the sketchy dreams that filled my head before then had finally become solid, well-carved paths in my mind. My background, my intellect, and willingness to dedicate my life to what I believed to be a good cause, made what I was starting to do as easy as it was painful.

Ever since I was a little boy, I loved to study — especially math, political science, and civics. Even before I was old enough to start first grade, I read everything I got my hands on including the newspapers. My mother was a librarian at my elementary school. She worked until 4:00 every day, but since I got out at 2:00, I walked home alone each afternoon. I had lots of time to myself. I enjoyed being alone, except when it rained. I didn't mind the rain itself; it was the fear of flooding that frightened me. The overflowing rivers and silent swelling of the ground petrified me.

I had few friends back then, and, like me, they preferred to be alone. I was the perfect bookworm and I didn't care if everybody knew it. I fit the part. At my high school graduation, I weighed 145 pounds, I was five feet six inches tall and wore heavy glasses. I had a slight stammer to my speech and considered it a compliment that no one paid any attention to me.

Growing up, my dad divided his time between Winston Salem, Washington, and Oak Ridge Tennessee. He would be gone months at a time. He made himself disgustingly wealthy by developing and manufacturing things for the Department of Defense, like barometric fuses used in high altitude bombs, and other stuff he couldn't talk about.

My favorite heroine was my mother's housemaid, a woman named Hagar. I spent so much time with her that my mother claimed I had picked up a Negro accent. My favorite hero was Edward R. Murrow, a native of Winston Salem, whose voice I listened to on the radio every night.

After the War, everyone at Chapel Hill believed they were there to learn how to change the world in some way. I was no different, just maybe a little more focused and a hell of a lot smarter.

When I started my graduate work at UNC, I lived alone, off campus, in a very large apartment. My favorite color was white, and I painted every room as close to pure, flat white as I could. Even the dining room furniture was white. I treated the wood floors with a dark teak stain. The light Carolina blue cushions on the couch matched the pillows on the dining room chairs. Those were the only spots of color in the apartment. The reason I chose to live in an apartment just off campus was I became a member of the Communist Party, and we needed a place away from downtown Chapel Hill to hold frequent meetings, and I was honored to use my apartment.

Of course, my family cut off all association with me

once I announced my membership in the Party. I think
Dad was more afraid it would damage his business, than
concerned about my reputation; however, he saw to it that
I was sent a substantial monthly allowance. I don't regret
joining the Party, but I regret the fact that I never saw
my Dad again after that. I never had a chance to explain
why I did what I did and what it was like to be part of a
revolution that had the potential to save us all from the rot
of capitalism.

On my first morning of graduate school, it took only
an hour to register for all my classes. I spent the rest of the
day in the back rooms of the *Community Book Store* where
the Party secretly maintained a semiofficial office. We had
a workroom, two desks and files, and a printing room
where we produced all our flyers and pamphlets. I had
worked in the bookstore since the end of my freshman
year in 1939. That's when I learned how to use the printing
equipment in the back rooms. We had a rotary press, a
letterpress, and a linotype machine. The equipment was
old, but we managed to keep it all running.

I worked through lunchtime that day, and by 4:30, I
was famished and decided to get a quick bite down the
street. The front sales area was still packed with students
finishing their checklists of required books. The three new
girls we had hired were doing their best, but the first day
of a semester at any bookstore near a university is almost
overwhelming. So I lingered in the store for a while to
help. We sent the last group of students out the door at six
o'clock, our usual closing time. Trish, the youngest and
smallest of the workers, sat down, closed her eyes, and let
out a long silent breath.

"It's not like this every day. G-Give it a week; it'll be

pretty easy," I said.

"I'm exhausted," Trish replied.

"I understand. Just rest as long as you need to, and when you feel like it, you can look around and pick out a few b-books for yourself?"

"Really?"

"Go ahead and enjoy the store …C-closing time doesn't apply to us."

Francis had told me all about Trish and how he thought she would learn to fit in. Her high school teacher, Elisabeth Ward, who worked with us for several years had become a loyal Party member. She had a brother who worked at the national headquarters in New York; consequently, she became a good conduit of information—to and from the headquarters.

After about fifteen minutes, Trish looked a little more rested and I asked, "Are you hungry?"

"Yes!"

"Let's go down the street. I missed lunch and I'm starving."

"That would be great. Thank you so much."

"Cynthia and Carole will close down the register and finish locking up. They've been working for us all summer and know the routine."

After dinner, we returned to the bookstore, and I straightened up some pamphlets while she looked through the shelves. She was a short, unassuming, likable girl. She wore a plain cotton dress with a light-blue flower print, flat shoes, and either no makeup or very little—exactly the way I pictured a girl who grew up on a North Carolina farm should look.

"I want to buy these for myself," she said placing a

stack of books on the counter.

"Good! And you will get a special d-discount because you work here."

"Oh, thanks! How much of a discount?"

I slid her pile of books toward her and said, "They're all paid for."

"What?"

"Yes, they're on me today."

"Oh, I couldn't ask you to do that?"

"You didn't. I just want…uh…t-to."

"Again, I thank you so much."

"We're just glad to have you here."

I placed on her stack a copy of a small book that I had just published.

She read the front and back covers carefully, then asked, "*William Logan*, Is that you?"

"Yes."

"Will you please sign it for me?"

"Yes, but if I do, you have to promise to…to like it." That was the first time I saw her face light up. She had a glow that shined through the slightest smile. "What's it about?" she asked.

"Civics. It explores different and fresh ways to look at government."

"Oh, I've never even thought about that sort of thing at all."

"That's great! You are the kind of person I want to read it."

"I'll start reading it right away."

Jack Hemphill

# CHAPTER FOUR

## TRISH
### SEPTEMBER 1946

Two weeks went by before I had a chance to meet our boss, Mr. Francis Schoberg. I stood at attention while he sat at his desk.

"Your name is Patricia Basil?

"Yes, Sir, but everybody calls me Trish."

"What kind of name is Basil?"

"I don't know. It's just a name."

"I'm asking where it came from."

"You mean what country?"

"Yeah."

"My brother tells me it comes from England and means *brave*."

"Are you brave?"

"Yes. Lem, my brother, says I got too much of it for my own good."

"You've been recommended to us by your high school English teacher. She used to work here. She said that you are very well read for someone your age."

"I love to read."

"What do you read?"

"Books."

"I mean what kind of books?"

"Oh everything, I like books about interesting people, mysteries, books that talk about other countries. I like drama."

"Name some of the books."

"Oh, I have my own collection at home. I've got the *Anne of Green Gables* series, a mystery called *The Secret Garden*, *The Sun Also Rises* by Hemingway, *Murder on the Orient Express*, a bunch of romance books you probably haven't heard of, a book about a wolf called *White Fang*, a book named *Gulliver's Travels* about going to unknown places."

"Did you like *Gulliver's Travels*?"

"Yes, my aunt gave it to me for Christmas. It was interesting, but kind of crazy."

"Can you tell me why Gulliver was so unhappy at the end of the book?"

"Well, he traveled all over the world and couldn't find a single country he wanted to live in. I think he was unhappy because he just wouldn't conform to other people's odd rules and so he ended up living alone with horses.

"What do you think would make him happy?"

"I don't know…maybe learning to live with strange laws and a different way of life."

"Good observation," he said. "Did you ever read anything by William Faulkner?"

"No, but I've heard of him, and I saw some of his books on a shelf out front."

"He was a good friend of the owner of this store. Spent a lot of time here, even in this very room." Trish glanced around the room.

"Look on the wall by the front door for an old photo of him standing in front of this building."

"Oh yes, I've seen it; I didn't know who it was."

Francis then asked who I wanted to win the presidency in the 1948 election. I told him I didn't know because I couldn't tell them apart, and the only president I had ever known was Roosevelt. He asked about what my dad did for a living, and if anybody in my family served in the military. He asked me questions that made no sense, and it went on for a half hour or so.

In a way, Mr. Schoberg frightened me, and in a way, I felt sorry for him. I found out later that he was from New Jersey. His graying hair was long, full, and he combed it straight back. His eyes were dark and his nose dominated his face. He had an accent I had never heard before. Although his voice was strong, it had a high, almost nasal, penetrating sound.

I was happy that I had two young women to work with. They were in their junior year at UNC. Cynthia Caldwell was a history major, and Carole Blythe was studying English. Even though they were only two years older than me, they each seemed more like my mother than girls my age. They attended Women's College in Greensboro for their first two years before transferring to UNC. They lived close to each other in Spencer Hall, the only women's dormitory on campus.

I loved my new life — not that I didn't miss being home during the day — but I needed to see more than just the farm, and Lem never thought of me as anything beyond a kid sister. I was so glad he let me drive the car to work. He preferred his truck almost all the time. But now and then, he had to use the car, and on those days, he didn't mind driving me into Chapel Hill and dropping me off around 7:00 AM, an hour before the store opened. Some mornings after dawn I spent my extra time walking around the UNC campus pretending I was a student. I enjoyed it so much I strolled the campus every morning, It was a gigantic and beautiful university. Every building was built with old bricks saturated with the fragrance and energy of thousands of students who lived there and learned everything about the world—everything I always wanted to know. Even at that hour, there were early-bird students scurrying across the yards and under the trees between the old structures. I felt like I was exploring a different country. I started bringing my breakfast in a bag, with a container of hot coffee. I found a spot in front of Graham Memorial Hall where I snuggled against one of the massive stone columns and watched the rising sun turning the tops of the trees orange in the big open yards around me.

It only took a few weeks before I met a new friend. He had long legs, wiry black fur, and was probably a descendent of every breed of dog in America. Each morning I brought a bag of dinner scraps and placed it on the Graham Hall porch floor behind the first column on the right. That way I could talk to him while he gobbled up his breakfast, and no one would see our secret rendezvous—which had become a morning ritual five days a week. I don't know what he did for food on the weekends, but I always brought him extra food on Monday mornings. It didn't take long before my little dog friend would be waiting for me, sitting beside his column before I arrived.

I usually sat with the dog until nearly 8:00, then we strolled around the crisscross walkways in the center of the campus and finally toward the bookstore. By that time, the paths were flowing with students wearing sleepy faces and trying to wake up enough to find their first class. I told Cynthia and Carole about my new friend, and occasionally, one or both of them joined me on the steps. Spencer Hall, where they lived, was close enough to Graham Hall for them to smuggle scraps of sausage, bacon, and sometimes scrambled eggs wrapped in a handkerchief, or in a small bag. Cynthia said she had seen him a few times around campus. Playing with that dog was the first thing outside of the shop we did together as friends, and I gradually became more comfortable with them. They were either starting to understand my weird humor, or they were being extremely kind to me. Both had classes all morning and sometimes the dog and I walked with them to their classroom buildings. After a while, some of the boys recognized us as the *girls from the bookstore*. We saw them almost every day. And they each gave us nods and said, "hello" in their deepest southern voices.

My first job each week was to straighten the shelves and place newly ordered books in their proper categories. I loved to work on book displays in the windows each morning while sunshine filtered through the giant willow oaks that covered the campus across the street. Until the cold weather set in, I picked flowers on my farm for the small tables around the store and for the windows. I tried to explain to Lem what a happy place it was, and how I was meeting so many interesting and smart people. Working with books inside a store for eight hours a day was his idea of hell, so at dinner time we mostly talked about ducks.

The front of our store looked directly across the center

of the UNC mall that stretched from Franklin Street all the way across campus to the Old Well beside Cameron Street. Every hour a bell chimed and students obediently flooded out of the buildings and marched down each crisscrossing path, creating a picture of perfectly structured chaos, but it was done in such a routine manner that the students passed through each other with orchestrated precision.

Standing in the bookstore in the morning sunshine, surrounded by books, looking across the threshold of a great American university and watching the hourly celebration of learning, made that fall one of the happiest times of my life.

I didn't know how ignorant I was, and I was oblivious to what was going on in the rooms behind the shop. Despite all I had read and studied, my mind was mostly a blank page begging for someone to write on it, and my new friends at the store were more than eager to start scribbling. Communism, to me, was nothing more than a subject debated by men with deep, authoritative voices on nighttime radio. I never thought I wanted to know anything more about it—until that fall.

# CHAPTER FIVE

## LEM
### SEPTEMBER 1946

My bedroom window stayed open all year round. I left a wooden block at the base of the window to hold it at least two inches above the sill. The ducks are usually quiet after dark unless they are disturbed by a fox or raccoon looking for a quick meal. The gates to all pens were always latched, but that never stopped a determined, hungry critter from digging his way under the fence.

A cool front finally broke the long Indian summer. A light rain and a light breeze made it easy to slip into bed a little early. The ducks quieted down as soon as the sunset. I brushed my cheek across the pillow and remembered nothing else until somewhere in my dream, I heard a frightened squawk. It must have echoed in my head for a couple of minutes before I awoke enough to realize the sound was coming through the open window.

Ducks are usually silent at night; however, when they sense an intruder, they make a racket so loud even I couldn't sleep.

As always, my coveralls were hung on the bedpost and my fully loaded Remington rifle and my leather boots were kept by the back door. And within thirty seconds

I flew down the hill to rescue my troops. I also had two flashlights taped to a steel Army surplus helmet. The chin strap kept it secured on my head while I ran.

The four-legged burglars, however, had disappeared into the black night without a trace, except a trail of white feathers scattered in front of one of the pens. When I arrived, the ducks were running back and forth and in circles, but as I walked toward the trail of feathers, the ducks pressed against the chicken wire of each pen to watch me and wait for my reassuring voice.

"It's okay now little duckies, the bad guys are gone. I'm here. You can go back to sleep." I continued talking loud enough so all the ducks in all the pens could hear me. I unlatched the gate of the pen where I found most of the feathers and looked around for who might be missing. The ducks followed me. I noticed a white flutter behind one of the nesting cubicles. It was little Samantha running back and forth flapping her wings, and I knew right away her mate had been nabbed by a fox or some other predator. I carefully lifted her into my arms and sat down with my back against the long stone wall. I continued stroking her back and wings until her shivering stopped. She turned her long neck to peek up at me every few minutes for the rest of the night. Somewhere in early morning, I fell asleep until the rising sun lit the pond like it was on fire.

To the right of the pond was a long marsh, and behind it was a thick forest that wrapped the side and back-half of the pond. I knew most of the creatures that loved the taste of ducks were hidden in that forest waiting for the right time to grab another meal.

Samantha had been still and quiet all night, but when I put her down, she let out such a loud squawk. It woke the other ducks who joined her as if they were all remembering the tragedy only a few hours earlier.

I scooped her up in my arms and carried her back up the hill to my house. She waddled circles around the kitchen while I made myself some toast and coffee. It was still a little earlier than my usual schedule, but since the ducks were all up, I opened the kitchen screen door wide enough for Samantha and me to walk outside together, around the house, and down the hill to the storage shed behind the pens. She continued to shuffle beside me as I spread breakfast in all the feeding troughs. Samantha wouldn't eat until I picked her up and placed her at one of the troughs. While she ate, I filled the drinking troughs and the bathing containers.

I thought if she ate with the ducks, she would rejoin the flock, but she followed me around all day with her right wing bumping the outside of my left calf. Again, I held open the mudroom door and the kitchen door wide enough for both of us to walk through together. She found a small dark nook under my mudroom sink and waddled into it thinking it was a nest built only for her. I dashed down to my barn and returned with an armload of fresh straw, which I scattered over half the room including her little nest underneath the mudroom sink. She took to it right away and I think she felt comfortable watching my feet as I walked around the room.

The following morning, she toddled beside me to the feeding areas again and ate a good duck breakfast. After a week, Samantha was as comfortable in the mudroom and kitchen as she was in any other part of the farm.

I always maintained the outside of the house exactly the way Mom had it, but the inside was starting to look more like a bachelor's house. Trish never said a word about it knowing how much I enjoyed making the changes that matched my personality.

Bobcats, hawks, foxes, raccoons, and snakes were always circling our farm watching for opportunities for free dinners. I shot my rifle at least once a week, either at night-creatures or at targets during the day. Every time I got a good clean kill, I took it to a guy named Grier Green, a taxidermist who lived two miles down the road. In the back of my house was a room full of beautiful stuffed raccoons, foxes, bobcats, and one copperhead. They looked so alive they startled me a little bit every time I walked into their sanctuary. The room had no windows and the only light came through the living room doorway that provided just enough glow to see the stuffed critters scattered around the room. On top of a wood box in the darkest corner, the copperhead was fixed in a coiled position with his head cocked back ready to strike. When the lights were out, all that could be seen of him were his two glass eyes shining and staring constantly at anybody that walked into the room. On the walls of my living room, I had two hawks, two weasels, and a boar's head. On the long wall, above the fireplace, hung a golden eagle with its wings stretched out to its full seven feet spread, clearly the most commanding figure in the room.

I had a great aim with my rifle and my pistol, and I would have been a good soldier in the war, but the Government gave me a deferment because of my status as a farmer. I had no fear of fighting, but with Dad gone, my job was to take care of the family and the farm.

# CHAPTER SIX

## WILL
## OCTOBER 1946

Francis had been asking me how well I thought Trish would fit in. I suggested that we have an informal meeting with her to see if she had any political preconceptions, or was she a blank slate? I arranged for him to come to the bookstore near 6:00 on a Thursday afternoon. I usually worked until well after closing time anyway with my school studies and with my work for the Party. Trish always stayed after hours putting things away and locking up.

Francis Schoberg was six feet tall and four feet around. He grew up in Summerville, New Jersey, and even though he had attended college in the South, he never bothered to polish off his Jersey accent. He was older than me, and it was hard not to be impressed with his knowledge of what was going on in the country, and his opinions about changes needed to be made with our government and our culture. I don't know how long he had been a member of the Party, but he was well connected with headquarters in New York and had attended several intensive training sessions up there.

My parents would have thought of him as their idea

of the perfect New Yorker—overweight, olive skin, loud, fast-talking, aggressive Yankee. But in spite of our differences—and we had many—he was brilliant and sometimes inspiring. When I was around him, I forgot about my awkward, halting, measured manner. Those things didn't matter anymore, and I learned to be comfortable around him most of the time, even though we didn't agree on some of the changes taking place within the Party.

After Trish had locked up that night, I called her into the back room. Francis wanted to talk with her a little more. If she was nervous, she contained it well.

"Where do you live, Trish?" Francis asked before she sat down and without any explanation why he wanted to talk with her.

"I live about ten miles from here," she said softly, but clearly.

"I think you told me your family runs a duck farm?"

"Yes."

"Who runs it now?"

"My brother does."

"I can tell a lot about people from the places where they grew up and what they do for a living. A duck farmer is a good thing."

"What would be a bad thing?"

"A banker, a politician, a developer, things like that."

"Why?"

"Money. They love money. It's what they're made of."

"And that's bad?"

Francis didn't answer her question, but turned toward me and lowered one eyebrow—his sign of disapproval.

"How many ducks on your farm? He asked."

"About six hundred."

"You ever grow attached to any of them?"

"Of course."

"How do you feel about sending them to market and having them slaughtered?"

"I feel *awful* about it, but my brother takes care of all that kind of stuff. I don't watch, and I don't let myself think about it.

"How have you managed not to think about it?"

"I worked in the incubation area and the brooding pens, and I just stayed on those things, and Lem never mentions that terrible part of his work."

"You know what he's doing; why doesn't it bother you?"

"Yes I know, but like I said, I can't let myself think about it.

"But you let him do it."

"Yes, I have to. We wouldn't have a farm if Lem didn't do those things."

Francis glanced at me again, but this time with a hidden smile. Trish wrinkled her forehead as if she didn't understand why he was asking those questions.

"Tell you what," Francis said as he raised his hands just enough to turn his palms upward. "Go with us tomorrow morning. We're driving to a factory outside of Durham. We're going to meet and talk with the workers about what they need. You know, hear their story. Why don't you come with us?

"Sure, it sounds exciting."

Francis took another half hour and talked about the workers he helped in unionized factories up North. Trish seemed interested but made no comment. We all agreed to meet at the store at 10:00 in the morning. Francis left and I stayed while Trish swept the store. Once we were outside, she stopped as if she had forgotten something, then said, "Will…" looking straight at me, she asked, "Are you two communists?"

Since the day I first met her, I thought about all the ways I could explain what communism is, why she should not be afraid of it, why she should not be afraid of us, and what it could do for her. But as usual, I stammered for a moment, and she, out of kindness or pity, recaptured the conversation.

She said, "I know nothing about communism except what I've read in my high school books or heard on the radio."

I told her that much of what she heard, was probably not true, even though I knew the Party made a lot of mistakes in the past, and I told her if she came with us in the morning, she would see what we are capable of doing.

She seemed satisfied with that answer and smiled. I could tell she was really looking forward to our adventure. I thought she was the kind of person who, once she got a taste of something, would always want more.

# CHAPTER SEVEN

## TRISH
## OCTOBER 1946

In our part of the state, thunderstorms spring out of nowhere, dumping waves of water on everything. On my way to town, the rain blew so hard, it was impossible to see much through the windshield; however, I didn't slow down. I left the farm an hour early to make sure I was there before he arrived, but by the time I got there, Will was already waiting in his car parked in front of the store.

My umbrella was useless. As soon as he saw me, he got out of his car and we both ran toward the building. Water gushed off the edge of the awning creating a river of white bubbles flooding across the sidewalk. We jumped over the stream and took refuge under the store's covered entrance. The storm pounding the streets and sidewalk was so loud it was difficult to talk, except in short bursts. After a while, he leaned close to me and shouted, "We better go inside and sit it out."

"Not just yet," I yelled back. "I love the sound of storms like this...like it's washing everything!"

"Washing?"

"Yes, nothing else makes me feel that way...but on days like this...everyone and everything gets drenched...

and there's nothing anyone can do about it...except watch and enjoy it...Everything else stops and it feels great.Ya know what I mean?"

"No," he said as loud as he could, "I never liked rain, especially hard rain like this. It worries me."

"It what?"

"Scares me!"

I said, "Looks like Francis's going to be late." He glanced back at me and made a motion with his head toward the door. That was my cue to unlock it. We went in. I immediately made coffee. It was a football weekend, and the store was always closed for home games. I never cared for the sport. It made no sense to me at all. Why so much screaming? What were they accomplishing? Will said he felt the same way. We talked for nearly two hours. He told me about projects they were working on including two more mills in Chatham County and in Alamance County, and the long ongoing project with the workers of Reynolds Tobacco in Winston Salem.

He said, "I know that all this activity with the mills may sound a little c-crazy and even a little wicked, but it's not. Our motives are to do whatever we can, to give these people some hope that they can improve their working conditions and earn better wages."

"That sounds great to me."

"We never know how these things will turn out, so don't let anything that happens today worry you or intimidate you. I think you're going to be very g-good at this, Trish."

I didn't know what he meant by that, but I couldn't wait to find out.

Francis finally arrived with a man named Gill Holstrum,

and we all dashed back across the sidewalk through the continuing deluge to our cars. Francis led the way with Holstrum sitting beside him. Two young women sat in the back seat. They were UNC students and new recruits into the Party.

The rain blew straight into our windshield as we crept along the back roads of Orange County. For the first half of the trip, Will concentrated so hard on driving that we didn't talk at all. I watched the exploding patterns of rain on the glass in front of me, and how perfectly beautiful they were before being instantly destroyed by the wipers' stroke, only to reappear in new patterns waiting to be smashed. I loved the powerful sound of thousands of drops hitting our car and the defiant blades pounding with the rhythm of a heartbeat.

I was on an adventure beyond Hillsboro with men and women I barely knew. Before that morning, Hillsboro was as far north as I had ever been. We followed Francis all the way to Durham where we were joined by two other cars carrying seven or eight men and one woman. I found out later that the woman's name was Rebeca. I did not know her, but I had seen her in the bookstore frequently. From there, we headed back toward Hillsboro.

As we got closer to our destination, Will talked about the poor conditions and poor wages at the mill, and how the workers needed help confronting the owners. It never occurred to me that employees had the right to make demands for better working conditions. It was hard to picture what we could do for the workers, and I had no idea what to say to them or how to start talking to them. But I was excited with the thought of being part of something totally different from anything I had ever done.

A high fence with an open gate appeared through the rain-soaked windshield. In the mist, the mill looked like a long gray ghost. We parked in a narrow lot, hoping the storm would finally pass. The tall one-story brick building had two rows of ten-foot-high windows, one above the other, running the length of the building. A pair of wood doors stood open at either end of the mill. Four steep concrete steps with no landing at the top cascaded from the open doors to a concrete sidewalk below. A single sign above each door said, EMPLOYEES ONLY.

Francis and Will talked with the workers in each car. Around three o'clock a man in work clothes walked out of the mill and, without looking at us, hustled around the back side of the building. Francis and Will followed him and were gone about an hour and a half. When they returned, they both talked again to our workers still sitting in the cars. Will finally came back to his car and gave me a quick report.

At exactly five-thirty, a bell at either end of the building rang for about fifteen seconds. Will handed me a pack of leaflets and said, "Okay, that's our signal." We got out of the car and walked to the front gate while the other men stood in the parking lot. The rain had nearly stopped, but the sky was still churning various shades of gray. My stomach, heart, and head throbbed with excitement. Employees streamed out of the building. Negros and white workers came out at the same time, but most of the Negros exited from the door farthest from the front gate. Some workers walked straight to parked cars in the lot and were approached by our people who gave them handouts. Others trudged toward us on their way to the gate. They had just finished a nine-hour day with a half-hour lunch break. Although they came out of the building in small clumps, most walked across the lot by themselves with their eyes fixed on the ground. They didn't notice us at first. All men wore work clothes, flannel or cotton shirts, and blue jeans or chino pants with rolled-up cuffs. The women wore plain cotton print dresses and comfortable shoes.

Will wasn't a fluid speaker and had his share of stumbles, but he spoke softly and reinvented his words every time he talked to a different worker. He never sounded like a salesman, and I think they trusted him immediately. Everyone stopped to hear what he had to say and took the leaflets we handed to them.

I had not seen or read the message on the pamphlets before Will gave me a handful. During the short walk from the car to the gate, I scanned the writing on the front and back. It described in simple language the same points I heard Will explaining to them. They were things all mill workers needed to hear: collective bargaining, fair working hours, fair distribution of pay, and better working conditions. Will explained that his organization was helping workers in other mills and plants all over the state and getting great results. He said that if they would like to know more about it or knew some of their fellow workers who would like to talk about it, they should fill out the information on the back of the handout and send it to him or call the phone number at the bottom of the form.

Will had a special way of evaluating the people and I could tell he was looking for a certain type of worker. He let some of them walk by with not more than a nod, but he approached others and asked them questions before telling them why we were there, and what we could do

Jack Hemphill

for them.

The last person Will stopped was a Negro woman with an expression fixed hard as stone. Her lips were drawn tight into a perfectly straight line across her face. At Will's signal, I handed her a leaflet and then stepped back for him to talk. His voice and his stride were like an undertaker greeting the bereaved in his parlor. I couldn't hear all that he said and I couldn't hear any of her replies. When he finished, they both turned away from the gate and started toward his car. He glanced back at me and gave a little motion with his head that said, *follow me*.

He didn't introduce us until we all got into the car. Her name was Betty Jones, and she insisted on sitting in the back. I stretched one elbow over the back of my seat so I could look at her and talk while Will followed directions to her house. She kept the conversation going nonstop, and her voice grew stronger and friendlier as we traveled. She asked about the other mills that had been in the same situation and run by the same type of owners. When she asked what the name of his group was, I looked at him wondering what answer he would give. I was slightly embarrassed that I never thought to ask how he would answer that question before we got to the mill.

"The name *of* our group is, *ALL*," he said, "It stands for *American Labor League*." I knew he made it up, but the woman seemed comfortable with it and continued talking more about her personal life.

"Got me three children," she said. "My oldest, she takes care of the other two when I'm at work."

"How old is she?" I asked.

"She's twelve."

"And the other two?"

42

"My boy's six and my little girl's five."

"No dad around?"

"No. None of 'em stuck around."

"Your oldest is not in school?"

"Nope, can't. She gotta take care of the others. I got no way of makin' no money if I stay home, ya know?

"Yes, of course."

"*Do* you make enough money?"

She shook her head back and forth with deliberate strokes, then looked at me. In spite of the clouds, light still radiated through the windshield and flowed over the dark, smooth skin on her face. I had not, until that moment, noticed how strong she looked and, at the same time, how pretty she was.

"Betty, by now, you know why we're here, d-don't you?" Will said.

"I heard you say you can help us, but I still can't see how."

"We'd like to meet with some of your friends from w-work, and talk about ways to make changes."

"They not gonna let you meet with us at work!"

"No, I understand, but if we can find a place to gather for just a brief meeting, we can explain what we do and how we can help."

"Don't know where that might be."

"Sometimes we meet at a worker's house, and sometimes we find other places like a local church."

"If you turn right here we'll be at my house in just a minute, but you gonna see why we can't have no meetin' there. My house is just like all these other cracker boxes around us. I'm at the top of the hill on the left." She was right. Dozens of houses were scattered over two rolling hills around us. Each house was obviously built from the same set of plans, not one deviated from the others in any detail, size, color, or absence of landscaping.

All three children were on the front steps playing and waiting for their mom. We stopped in front of the house, but the children could not see her through the car's dark windows. Not knowing who we were, they ran inside. Betty opened her door and called out, "Where you little scaredy-cats think you're goin'?"

The front screen door flung open and all three ran to her. After receiving a good mamma hug, the youngest ran to me. I got out of the car, knelt on one knee, and she hugged my neck.

"What's your name, sweetheart."

"Christine," she said.

"Hello, Christine. I'm Trish. You're a pretty little girl, aren't you?

"I don't know."

"Well, I'm here to tell you that you are."

Christine giggled then joined the other two forming a straight line. They looked at me as if I had fallen into their yard from space. They wore jeans that were probably clean at the start of the day, but by then, a full layer of children's grime from playing in the yard, sitting on the porch, and rolling on the damp ground covered all knees and rumps. They also wore pullover cotton shirts and no shoes.

"You can see my little place isn't big enough to have no meetin's, but I could talk to my preacher on Sunday about lettin' us have a little group meetin' over there for a little while.

"That would be excellent, Betty," said Will. You've got my telephone number on the paper Trish gave you. Just call me and we can talk about when to set it up."

The children, still standing in front of their mother, smiled at us. I waved and Christine waved back.

Will wanted to check on the rest of our team back at the mill. We hoped they were still there. Before we got within one hundred yards of the place, we saw both entrance and exit gates were blocked with official looking cars. Because of the line of trees between the road and the mill fence, we couldn't see into the parking lot at all. Will drove past the mill and stopped his car on a little turnaround on the far side of the street. We ran back to the gates. Six police cars were scattered around the parking lot with red lights flashing in a random pattern causing the side of the mill to look like it was on fire. The first person I recognized was Francis, whose hands were cuffed behind his back, face down, over the hood of a police car. I wanted to help him, but Will stopped me from running through the gate. I couldn't find Gill Holmstrum or the other guys anywhere, but I did notice several mill workers were also handcuffed in the back seat of two police cars and one was face down on the ground.

A uniformed policeman walked straight toward us and said, "Get off the property and move on or you're gonna join 'em." We didn't answer but ran straight back to the car and left. No more than a quarter mile down the road, we passed an ambulance speeding toward the mill.

"What the heck was that all about?" I blurted out as we watched the flashing light disappear in the mirror. The rainstorm from that morning was long gone and sunlight had broken through the clouds. Neither of us felt like talking. When I adjusted the visor to shield my eyes from the sun, I saw my hand shaking. I stretched out both hands together. They trembled like spring leaves in the wind. I buried them in my lap before Will noticed how frightened I was.

We had no way of finding out what happened until Holstrum showed up at the store the following morning. He spent the night at the Hillsboro Police station answering questions but was finally released without charges. Francis, however, was booked on several charges. Holstrum told us that while he and Francis were talking to some of the workers, one of the managers ran out and started yelling and called them commies, and told them to get off the property. Francis tried to argue back and the manager grabbed him and shoved him toward the gates. Francis, who was twice the manager's size, threw him down. That's when four or five line-managers came running out holding wooden spindles like clubs in their hands. Each of the spindles was about a foot long. The first line-manager that reached Francis knocked him to the ground. That's when a half-dozen or more workers ran out of the building and grabbed some of the managers and dragged them back into the mill. More employees armed with swinging spindles joined in and charged the crowd. Holmstrum said it only took a few minutes for the Hillsboro police to swarm the lot, and stop the fighting. He didn't know how many were arrested and made no mention of the bandage across the back of his skull.

When Holstrum finished, Will shook his head and quietly said he was sorry it happened and hoped Francis was okay. An awkward silence followed. The last thing I expected at that moment from Will was silence, and I guess Holmstrum expected something more from him too. Finally, after taking a deep breath, Will said, "I'll contact our attorneys to get on the c-case. They'll have Francis out by sometime tomorrow. We've both been through this. I'm sure a condition of the bail will be that Francis will have to stay away from us, the Party, until his trial is completed."

That was all Will said about Francis that day. Will never went to see him and never inquired about how he was doing. It would be a long time before I understood why.

I threw out the only question still hanging in my mind, "What's a 'Commie'?"

Holmstrum fired back immediately, "*Communists*. He said we were *communists*."

"What a *stupid* thing to call us!" I cried out, thrusting my arms forward as if I were flinging water off my hands. Will and Holmstrum looked at me and wrinkled their foreheads. Lem always told me I never knew when to keep my mouth shut. I wanted to crawl under the table.

Will sat back and raised his eyes toward the ceiling waiting for Holstrum's response.

Holstrum said, "Trish...being called a commie is *nothing*. You have to understand: we're defenseless out there. We're all targets to the police, to the state government, the Federal government, and even the university. The first thing I do every morning, and the last thing I do every night is look out my window to see who might be watching me. Being in jail for a while may do Francis some good,"

•••

That day horrified me, electrified me, excited me, and

filled me with a desire to help people just like Betty and her family; however, I was beginning to fear that, sooner or later, I would have to fight like the men at the mill, and that was never going to happen.

# CHAPTER EIGHT

## LEM
## NOVEMBER 1946

The first weekend in November was cool. I wanted to take a few extra-long moments while the sun inched its way over the low-lying clouds on the horizon, but ducks need to be fed two times a day, and the feeding ritual starts at daybreak.

I stood on my porch a few minutes with a steaming cup of coffee and looked over the farm, the duck pens, the garden, and the ponds. My house sat on a hill and faced north-east, thirty-five feet above the ponds.

I never made Trish get up that early. She loved to sleep, and she waited for me to wake her almost every morning. Ever since she was old enough to wash ducklings, she spent almost all her weekends and all her time after school helping me with the flock. She was a hard worker and never had much time for friends. As far as I could tell, that never bothered her. I guess that's why I was surprised she wanted to work in that store.

I never imagined being anywhere but the farm, and I couldn't picture how I could have been any happier anywhere else. I was in the third grade when Dad died. I quit school to run the farm, but the truth is I was too big to fit in with the other boys at school.

Quincy had been working on the farm since before I was born, and I learned as much about raising ducks from him as I did from my dad. I can't remember a time when I didn't know him, and when I was a very young boy, I thought he was a member of the family. He never talked much while he was working, but he loved to tell good stories on his lunch break. With nothing but a sickle, Quincy could cut an acre of hay in a single day. I loved to watch him bundling the bales with his beefy black hands pulling the thick string so tight the bales bowed in the middle. Depending on the time of year, we needed him three to four days every week. He lived with his wife in a little house beside the Haw River within walking distance of our farm.

Years ago, my dad and Quincy rebuilt the pens. The roof over the new structure was supported with timber posts and beams, twelve feet on center. The long wall close to the pond was made of fine mesh wire fencing. The end walls and the long wall between the barn and the pens were made of fieldstone. This gave the ducks a place in the back of the structure to huddle and keep warm during winter months and stay safe from predators who were constantly seeking the weakest and most helpless in the flock. My dad always told me there were three kinds of predators. The first predators were snakes that came out of the ground and ate only duck eggs and little ducklings. The second predators were foxes, weasels, raccoons, and all the animals that came from the forest around us. And the third predators were the hawks and eagles that came from above.

The roof kept hawks and eagles from swooping down

and picking out unsuspecting ducks during the day. The walls and fences helped keep forest creatures from snatching the ducks every night; however, Dad never figured out a way to keep out the snakes.

Between the rear stone wall and the side of the barn, I built a long, narrow shed for duck feed. The feed was a mixture of cracked corn, wheat, and barley. It was expensive feed, almost good enough for people, but the ducks loved it and it made them healthy and fat. I kept my rifle close by all day long ready to shoot anything that didn't belong on my farm.

Jack Hemphill

# CHAPTER NINE

## LEM
## MARCH 1947

Trish gave me a map of the university and Chapel Hill with a star drawn beside the bookstore. I wanted to see where she worked and hopefully meet some of her friends, especially the guy named Will that she talked so much about.

I came into town near the end of the day and found a parking spot about thirty feet from the bookstore. The building was old but well-kept. I had to bend over a little as I walked inside to keep from bumping my head on the low door frame. I was surprised to see how many students were in the little shop. Trish was apparently in the back room, and I looked around the stacks and displays for a few minutes waiting for her. Because of my height, I was used to people staring at me. The chatter around the store noticeably quieted as I walked around the shop. Trish saw me when she stepped out of the back room.

"Lem! you're here," she said loud enough for everybody to hear. She signaled for me to come to the front desk where she introduced me to Jackie McDougal and Carole Blythe. I leaned over and shook their hands. Both women seemed a little intimidated by me, which was not unusual, but I tried to smile and speak in a soft tone. Trish always told me that my loud voice sometimes sounds more like a bear than a person.

"Nice to meet both of you," I said. They nodded back.

"Stand here for a moment while I get William," Trish said.

"I'll walk back with you." I didn't want to be left standing with the two girls.

"No, it's okay. He'll be right out," she said before disappearing into the back room. Again, I awkwardly smiled at the two women still standing at attention. I think it finally dawned on them that they had been staring at me, so they eased back to their work.

Will came from the back room following Trish who immediately introduced us.

The most honest thing I can say about Will is that he was a totally unimpressive man. When he looked up at me, the ridge of his eyebrows covered the top half of his eyes.

"Trish's told me a lot about you," I said. That's what everybody spits out at times like that.

"Oh?" he said.

"Well, I'm sure we're keepin' you from your work, and Trish wants to show me the campus," I said.

"Nice to m-meet you," he replied with a quick glance at me, then returned to his cave.

"I know what you're thinking," Trish said the moment we stepped onto the sidewalk.

"You told me he's a little different. He lived up to your description. But I don't care, I really don't, and I'm happy for you, as long as you like bein' here." Trish looked relieved at my answer and gave me a walking tour of the university. It was a really nice campus with lots of very different kinds of people and buildings everywhere, but I still couldn't help thinking that Trish was out of place in Chapel Hill. I couldn't remember, however, how long it had been since she looked that happy.

We walked past a maze of old brick buildings with students hustling in every direction. Trish tugged my sleeve and whispered, "That guy we just past!"

"What about him?" I asked.

"*That's* Charley Choo Choo Justice!" She acted like I was supposed to know the name.

"Who?"

"They call him Choo Choo."

"*Chook Choo?*"

"Yes!"

"That's a *baby's* name!"

"No, he's a big football player here, and sometimes he says hello to me," she said with a little smile.

"Well...I'm glad I got to see him." I was surprised she recognized him, and I was amazed how much she knew about the campus.

We passed an old well, an impressive bell tower, and more academic buildings.

Beside one of the buildings stood a covered shelter with a campus bulletin board packed with notices of events, and handwritten requests from students looking for rides home to different parts of the state. We stopped to see what was happening around campus. I listened to two students as they walked by laughing about their professor's quirky accent. I scanned a bulletin board just to see what her friends were doing and thinking. One note grabbed my attention. Across the top, it read,

"JOIN US AT THE COMMUNITY BOOKSTORE AT 10:00, EVERY SATURDAY MORNING FOR DISCUSSIONS AND DEBATES ON THE FUTURE OF COMMUNISM IN AMERICA."

"Look at this, Trish!" I said while I read the fine print. She didn't reply as if she didn't hear me. "Read this," I said again, "You won't believe it. Is that your bookstore?" She still didn't answer. "Trish, did you know this stuff was goin' on there?"

"Yes, I've heard people talking about it," she said quietly.

Students continued to walk by on all four sides of the little pavilion. My mind froze, and I couldn't form a single word. When I finally gained my composure, I whispered, "You don't know what you're doin' do ya?"

"Why do you *always* say that to me?"

"I don't. I don't *always* say that to ya."

"Yes, you either say it to me outright, or you think it. Either way, I hear it."

"Well then Trish, hear this: I know what I'm talkin' about, and you don't know what you have gotten into!"

Trish always had a way of broadcasting her anger before she let it go. She squinted, rolled her lips into a straight line, and took a long, deep breath through her teeth, but as she did, three students entered the shelter behind us. She exhaled and said, "Let's go." We walked back to the bell tower. She took another deep breath.

"Lem! I'm not your *kid* sister anymore. I'm a woman."

"You're just eighteen."

"*I'm a woman,* and I know what I'm doing."

"That's true, but you can't do this anymore. I'll find you another job."

"*You*? What kind of job?"

"Whatever it takes to save your damn life. Trish, you're not goin' to tell me you *knew* about this before ya started workin' here, are you?"

"I didn't know about it then."

"Good!"

"I didn't know about it before I got here, but it's not what you think."

"I think it's *communism*. What else do I need to know?"

"They're not bad people Lem and actually, they're very intelligent and interesting."

I stopped, and with both hands, held my head for a moment, as if I needed to keep it from exploding. "Is this that Will guy's doin'?"

"Lots of people do it."

"Ya gotta promise me you'll stay away from them *and* him."

"I can't do that!" she yelled at me for the first time since she was a young girl. She stood square in front of me. Her head was cocked back as she looked up into my face. My anger melted into sorrow. I knew she had no idea what she could lose. She pulled my arm as we walked around the rest of the campus. I pleaded with her to come back and work on the farm. She begged me to trust her, and not worry. We both knew the conversation was useless. She said the names of each building, but we didn't talk about much else after that. For the first time in our lives, we didn't know what to say to each other. She gave me a little hug and whispered a goodbye, then turned toward the store. I watched her walk away. She didn't look back.

Whenever I argue with someone, I usually spend the rest of the day going through mental debates and brilliant thoughts to trash their silly opinions echoing in my mind. But while driving back to the farm that day, I heard no thoughts, no arguments, no stupid voices— just a silent empty numbness, like someone had pulled a plug out of the back of my head, and it all drained out in the air and blew away.

Quincy had finished his chores early and fed the ducks their afternoon meal, and Samantha found me the moment I walked to the pens. The duck and I once again sat in the straw with my back to the stone wall and watched the trees fade into silhouettes against the night sky.

# CHAPTER TEN

## LEM
### APRIL 1947

Trish told me about meeting her dog friend each morning for breakfast behind the giant columns of Graham Hall. They had become good friends and the dog was obviously a stray, so she took off from work a little early one Friday afternoon and walked the campus looking for him. Somehow, *he* found *her*, and she coaxed him into her car and brought him home.

I built him a bed out of old wood crates and blankets and placed it in the corner of the kitchen. He was very timid at first, but he felt safe and quickly realized he had a new home. In time, he would learn to be totally obedient to us and willing to do anything Trish or I asked him to do. He and I were immediate pals. I named him *Bearcat* after the World War II fighter plane.

Samantha still slept at night in her nest in the mudroom. Bearcat had never seen a duck up close, and Samantha wasn't sure if he wanted to be her friend or wanted her for dinner. The first evening, Samantha chased him around the kitchen three times before I picked Bearcat up and held him in my arms far above Samantha's snapping yellow beak. After seeing the dog in my arms for a while, she calmed down and returned to her nest.

The following morning, I took Bearcat down the hill to the pens, and I made him sit outside and watch as I fed each group of hungry ducks. He barked and ran back and forth outside the pens, which made the flock nervous. Bearcat stayed outside the pens the rest of the week. After that, I took him in inside the pens on a rope leash. At first, he dragged all four of his paws, and I had to pull him into the pen, but when he saw the ducks running away from him and darting from one side of the pen to the other, he walked beside me with his head against my leg. I made him sit on the ground while the ducks reluctantly waddled to the feeding troughs and finished their breakfast. They looked at him between each bite.

He was a smart dog and learned his role on the farm quickly. The ducks got used to him as one of the farm family. Within a few months, he learned the smell of foxes, raccoons, skunks, and weasels, and made it his duty to go after them whenever he picked up even the faintest scent. The only times the critters were able to get into the pens without being detected were on extremely windy nights when the odors and the sounds of little digging paws were blown away.

Bearcat knew what time Trish usually came home from work, and we waited for her on the porch and listened for the sound of her car winding around the long gravel drive to our house. She always gave him a hug and he returned the greeting with licks across her neck.

His eyes were soft, kind, and dark brown. He constantly watched us to see what we needed and what he could do to help. We had no idea what his previous life was like, but I'm sure he couldn't believe his good fortune when he found Trish.

Besides being a constant companion, his biggest contribution was giving me advanced warning the moment someone or something came into the farm.

Jack Hemphill

# CHAPTER ELEVEN

## LEM
### MAY 1947

Linda's store had a tiny brass bell on the back of the front door. It had a sweet, delicate jingle—the kind of sound a woman would like. I always thought it should be more like a cowbell, but she liked the tiny one, and I didn't talk about it much. We had known each other ever since we were long, skinny children running around the farm.

At six-foot-three, she was, I'm sure, the tallest woman I ever knew and I loved to watch her walk. Even though she moved as fast as any man, including me, she always looked like she was gliding in slow motion. Linda preferred to wear slacks most of the time, but you could tell, even though her slacks, that she had unusually long, slim legs that moved her effortlessly across the floor. When she sat down, she intertwined her legs several times, like morning glories wrapping their way up a pole. She may have been the only woman I ever knew that felt comfortable walking beside me.

"Well, hello sugar," she said as the little bell announced me.

"Hey, Bean." That's what I called her because she had the figure of a string bean.

"Where ya been?"

"Where ya think?"

"Takin' care of ducks?"

"What else would anybody wanta do?" I said.

"Running a general store would be a good start."

"Too many people to deal with."

"Not right now; it's just you and me."

"That's the way I like it…Ya got any potatoes left?"

"Yep, I put the sacks on the floor near the back cooler."

"Carrots?"

"Same place."

"Onions?"

"Yes. Looks like you're making a stew," she said.

"Yep, duck, duck stew…except I'm not goin' to stew it. I'm gonna cook the duck part on the open grille."

"Why would you do that?"

"'Cause Trish will be late comin' home and I don't know exactly how to do real duck stew."

"Well darlin', if you do it on the *grill*, it's *not stew*."

"Okay, but I don't know how to do it in a pot."

"You need herbs."

"Why?"

"Makes it taste right. Makes it taste twice as good."

"Never learned how to do that."

"How 'bout you lettin' me come over and show you how?"

"You got the herbs?"

"I got everything. I got a *store*."

"Okay! I finish with the ducks about six."

"Gina's helping me at the store this afternoon, so I'll be there at five and prepare the meat. It'll be ready for you to start cooking by six."

"How long will it have to cook?"

"Hours."

"Oh...tell you what, come over on Saturday. We'll have all day for the stew. Jus' you and me. Trish has to work this Saturday."

"*All day* is the way to do it, and Saturday is my day off."

"Okay, great!" I said.

"I'll help you with those vegetables," she said as she eased around the counter. I let her walk in front of me so I could watch her graceful stride.

I paid for the groceries and we caught up on some old gossip. As I was leaving I said, "I probably need to tell you somethin'."

"What is it, sweetie?"

"There's a duck name Samantha that'll be sleepin' under the mudroom sink while you're there."

"Okay, good. I'll look forward to meeting her."

Saturday morning, I was putting pots and pans on the counter when I heard Bearcat barking. I glanced out the kitchen window and saw Linda closing her car door with her foot while balancing two canvas bags in her arms. Bearcat stood in front of her, sizing her up.

"I think I forgot to tell you, I also have a new dog," I said as I ran out the mudroom door.

The dog could tell from my voice that she was a friend, so he walked over to greet her with a sniff on her hand. She knelt down on one knee and patted his head.

Linda dumped her bags onto the kitchen table and started explaining all her magic ingredients: salt, pepper, olive oil, dried onions, thyme, butter, rosemary, bay leaves, mushrooms, small red potatoes, and carrots.

"I need for you to get out the duck meat and a big pot, but before we get started, I'd like to meet Samantha," she said.

"Ya just walked past her. Go back to the mudroom and look under the sink."

Linda quietly tiptoed across the straw and knelt in front of her. "Hello sweet thing," she said. Samantha quacked back.

"What a pretty nest!" She must have talked to her a full five minutes while I chopped carrots and potatoes. In a half hour, we had everything stewing away in the pot.

"It's time to let the ducks out of the pens for their romp around the yard," I said.

"Good! I finally get to meet the rest of your friends," she said.

Linda walked through the back door first. I followed but paused to let Samantha waddle into her place directly behind me. Bearcat was happy to be last. All four of us marched in single file to the pens.

"Okay all you duckies, *play time*," which is what I said every day when it was time for their exercise. Before we reached the front pens, half the flock squawked and quacked so loud Linda couldn't hear my warning to stand aside, but she got the message as I removed the lock on the first gate and the white avalanche flew past her into the yard. We went through the same thing with the second adult pen, but it was even louder and more frantic because they knew all the other ducks had gotten ahead of them.

I signaled for Linda to follow me to the young nestling pen. They, too, knew it was time for their swim, but they were more quiet and cautious.

We watched while the adult ducks scattered into the

grass area, the garden, and into the marsh. After a while, all at once, they started toddling toward the pond as if called by a voice only they could hear.

"You should see this from the top of the knoll," I said. We hustled back up the hill, paused for Samantha to catch up, then walked toward the ridge that jutted into the big pond. Even from there, we heard the constant duck chatter as they marched into the pond.

Linda and I sat in the grass. Bearcat nudged his way between Linda and me.

At the edge of the clearing, Samantha settled in a nearby nest of weeds while we watched the white army glide by silently, obediently in rhythm, with all heads held high in expectation of something unknown. As always, the flock glided in a counter-clockwise motion around the pond, pushing silver ripples through dark reflections of trees.

Linda almost never took her eyes off the flock. After a few minutes, she asked, "Is there one supreme leader of the flock?"

"Yes, it's always the biggest, toughest drake in the yard, however, he's got lots of competition every day."

"So, are they fighting all the time?"

"No, not all the time, but the leader has to assert his authority every day."

"Then, why do they all follow him so faithfully?"

"'Cause they believe he's the only one that can save them from the predators all around them."

"They all seem so peaceful right now."

"We separate the aggressive drakes when they're around ten weeks old, still in the broodin' pen. Sometimes they're marked with a dye. Most of them, as soon as they're full size, are taken live to the market, or slaughtered by

Quincy, and then sold."

"Wow, poor guys."

"Well, I know it's brutal; However, if a female duck is not layin' eggs regularly, she's taken to the market, too. We can't worry about that sort of thing, because we just do what's best for the farm. You know?

Three long wrinkles formed between Linda's eyebrows. I don't think she understood, or maybe she just didn't know I could be so blunt. The truth is, Trish and I suffered a little for every one we slaughter or send to the market. We always felt that way, but my job is to breed and raise these beautiful little birds for one purpose — to get them to market.

"So, the male ducks that get to stay should be pretty happy. I assume they get their pick of who they want to mate," she said.

"Well, that's what they think."

"You mean it's not true?"

"Actually, the female ducks choose who they want as a mate."

"So how well do the other drakes take rejection?"

"Oh, Bean, like all males! They can't accept it and it's a real problem. Female ducks that have no mate are very vulnerable and single drakes look for opportunities to trap the female ducks."

"You mean they…?

"Yes, a female duck on a farm like this has a higher chance of being raped than almost anything else in the animal world, and sometimes they're brutally injured, and sometimes they don't survive."

"Oh, my God! I had no idea. They're all so beautiful and gentle."

"Actually, *all* drakes and ducks have certain animal instincts planted deep inside, out of sight, just like the other creatures around the farm. But I'll tell ya what, I've been wachin' ducks my whole life. I've seen the brutal side, and I've seen another side too. Those who have mates are mates for life, and when a drake or a duck dies, its partner never stops mournin' and refuses to mate again. Also, when a duck is sick or injured, other ducks in the flock will understand her pain and keep her safe and warm at night until she recovers. I don't know where it comes from, but *that* kind of instinct isn't *animal*.

After a half hour, all four of us returned to the house. As soon as we stepped on the porch, we smelled the aroma of stew. It turned out to be the best duck stew I ever ate. Trish came in later but had already eaten dinner in Chapel Hill. After her usual chatter, mostly with Linda, Trish went to bed. There was plenty of stew left over, and we managed to fit the whole pot in the freezer. Linda and I relaxed in the porch chairs. A low yellow moon bounced off the pond.

We sat quietly for a few minutes, then Linda asked, "How's Trish? You told me she works hard."

"She works *very* hard. I didn't think she would last this long."

"What exactly does she do at the store that's so exhausting?"

I looked at the sky for a moment. She waited patiently for me to answer. "I went to Chapel Hill to see where she works and meet her friends."

"I know, but you haven't said much about it," she said.

"I've been wantin' to talk to you all afternoon."

"Why didn't you?"

"I just haven't figured out how to start."

"What could possibly be that bad? She's a good person. Whatever the problem is, I know she's going to be okay."

"Oh Bean, I wish I could say *you're right*, but the truth is I don't know. The few things she's said to me about it, and the little bit I saw that day, all tell me she's in trouble, and I don't know how to fix it. The *worse* feelin' in the world is *helplessness*."

"What did you see that makes you believe she's in that much trouble?"

"They're communists!"

"Who?"

"The people at the store."

"How would you know that?"

"She told me."

"Oh, my God! Are you going to get her out of there?"

"I wish I could, but she's dug in. You know what I mean?"

"It doesn't seem like her. "

"That's right! And that's what's botherin' me the most. She's *changin'*, and I don't know her anymore. I'm losing her."

For the first time, I realized how much was smoldering inside me.

Linda held my hand and we intertwined our fingers. I wrapped my arm around her, and we sat there until cool evening air moved us to the living room couch, where we stayed all night.

# CHAPTER TWELVE

## TRISH
### JUNE 1947

On certain Friday mornings, in the parking lot behind the store, we assembled into groups. Each group had a different mission and left with four to six cars at a time. I normally drove with Will, and our group was always the last to leave because Will wanted to speak to the workers in every car as they drove out of the parking lot. I noticed that those who participated in the Friday trips were the younger party workers, mostly students. The Friday events were the easy ones to accomplish. The more difficult tasks, like the union confrontations at Reynolds Tobacco, were always managed by more experienced people.

Even though only one-third of all the workers were members of the Party, we all believed in the cause. Will and Francis never doubted everybody's loyalty and sometimes gave responsible jobs to young, promising workers even to some that were not members.

On one Friday in August, Francis wanted me to go with him to Raleigh and asked me to drive my car. I thought it was odd, but I didn't ask why. We left before the other groups, and Francis gave me instruction to head for the Raleigh-Durham Airport. It was typical for Francis to keep information to himself until the last minute. After we were well out of Chapel Hill and heading up highway 54, Francis said, "We're going to have a special opportunity this morning to talk with someone on the National Committee."

"Will this be someone I've heard of?" I asked.

"Not just someone. We're picking up John Gates."

"Great...Who's John Gates?"

Francis breathed in slowly and deeply, then replied as if he could barely hold onto his patience. "He's one of the top ten leaders at Party Headquarters."

"In New York?"

He breathed in again, but not as deeply as before. "Yes, of course, and he has business in Raleigh. He'll be staying there for a few days."

"I'm looking forward to meeting him." I really *wasn't* looking forward to meeting him, but I knew that was what Francis wanted to hear.

"It's an interesting time for the CPUSA and for us in North Carolina," said Francis as he leaned against the door and hung his elbow out the window.

"Why?"

"Because we're really starting to make headway with our recruiting, and at the same time, the Feds are starting to enforce the Smith Act."

"What's the Smith Act."

"It's an act of Congress that allows them to persecute communists," he said using a fake, patient tone in his voice. "Gates is being investigated right now for violation of the Act."

"Why haven't I heard of that before now?"

"It came into law about eight years ago, but they're just

now starting to use it as a real stick to eliminate the Party. It's very controversial."

"Why is it controversial?"

"Because a lot of people in Congress feel threatened by us, and they don't know what to do—so they're grabbing at things, writing laws, and constantly revising them. Right now, there is a bill being drafted by a congressman from California, named Richard Nixon."

"I've never heard of him, either."

"He's just a congressman, but he's concerned that the Smith Act is driving the Party underground, and he thinks that would make it more dangerous. His bill will require every communist to register with the government."

"I think *his bill* would drive the Party underground faster," I said.

"Maybe so."

"Francis, are we picking up a *fugitive*?"

"No, he's not running from feds, not yet."

At the airport, Francis told me to wait at the front drive while he ran in and met Mr. Gates. Francis placed him in the front passenger seat and then sat in the back seat behind me. Mr. Gates turned out to be an interesting and polite person, with a beautiful, booming voice that would have been perfect for an audience outside or in a large auditorium, but not in the car. From his briefcase, he pulled a stack of papers and handed them to Francis. Francis looked at each one carefully and made a few marks with a pencil and handed them back. He directed me to highway 70 toward Raleigh. Francis asked about the latest FBI efforts to indict him. Just as Mr. Gates launched into a vigorous condemnation of FBI activities, Francis interrupted him and said, "Excuse me, John, but I've been checking behind us since we left the airport, and I think someone is following us."

Mr. Gates looked out the back window. "Oh yes, you're right. I've learned to recognize the government vehicles a mile away."

Francis looked back again and said, "I noticed he pulled in behind us when we left the airport and has not been out of sight ever since."

"Well, you asked about how the FBI investigation was going. I think this speaks for itself."

"Have they been watching you in New York?"

"Full time."

"I'll take care of him." Francis directed me to continue on 70, but to turn left on Morgan Street when we got to Raleigh. We passed the State Capital Building, and the government car remained about two blocks behind us. After a few more blocks, Francis told me to turn left again onto Person Street. It was a quiet, one-way road perfectly straight as far as I could see.

"Slow down and watch for him to turn on to this street," said Francis. The agent had momentarily lost sight of us, and he skidded slightly trying to round the turn onto Person Street. "Now stomp on the gas!" Francis shouted. I did, and as soon as we reached fifty miles per hour, Francis yelled again, "Now hit the brake, and turn the steering wheel slightly to the left."

"I can't, we'll crash into a pole or something!" I yelled.

"Do it. Now!" he said with such force I thought he might grab the wheel. So I slammed on the brake and turned the wheel slightly to the left. That was all it took to launch the car into a fishtail and start me screaming. We spun 180 degrees before the back wheels slammed into the curb on the left side of the road. The car stopped. I stopped screaming. I gripped the wheel and stared straight through the windshield. I didn't dare look at Francis and hoped he wasn't watching me trying to catch my breath.

"Now step on it again!" yelled Francis. Within a few seconds, we were flying 45 miles per hour, going the wrong way on a one-way street. I couldn't believe Francis was laughing. I don't remember ever being that afraid in my life, yet I continued to obey everything he said.

We zoomed past the gray car and, without stopping, we turned back onto Morgan Street. We lost sight of the car and he never found us again. Francis directed me to a road, called Boylan Avenue, on the south side of Raleigh, not far from the Dorothea Dix Hospital. We stopped in front of a large, white, two-story house with a covered porch wrapped around the front, accented by white wood rails and long vertical posts.

I said goodbye to Mr. Gates, and Francis escorted him into the house. Francis returned in about twenty minutes without Mr. Gates, and we headed back to Chapel Hill. Just outside the city limits, Francis noticed another escort was waiting for us. They immediately picked up the pursuit behind us, but this time a little closer. I'm sure the FBI already knew my car and license plate, and I didn't know how much they had been watching me before then, but I do know they started increasing their surveillance of me after that day.

I dropped Francis off behind the Store and started home. From that point on, I couldn't stop looking in the rear-view mirror about every thirty seconds.

Lem and I fixed dinner together that night: ham steak, rice, collards, and cornbread. I always felt a little better after eating cornbread stuffed with butter. As usual, Lem was quiet and, for once, I didn't feel like talking either. I needed a hug; I needed to cry, but I couldn't ask for either because what I did that day had to remain my secret.

Bearcat sat close to me that night.

# CHAPTER THIRTEEN

## TRISH
### JULY 1947

I was always glad when weekends came, not just because I usually didn't have to work at the store, but because I enjoyed helping with the flock. After Linda started coming around on Saturdays, I looked forward to my weekends. Other than the difference in our height, we actually had a lot in common. She enjoyed feeding the little guys in the afternoon, and she was always ready to help in the incubation and nestling pens. Unlike Lem, who talked as little as he could get away with, she was chatty. That means she was also a good listener which made Linda and Lem a good match.

July was always warm enough to produce enough insects and water plants to keep the ducks happy. Linda and Lem liked to collect eggs while most of the ducks were out. Bearcat stayed in the house until Lem and Linda finished their morning chores. Each nest had to be inspected for eggs every day, but Lem always skipped Fridays so Linda could do it with him on Saturdays. By then, the ducks had become used to Linda's face and didn't mind her lifting them off the nest for a moment while she checked for eggs. She and Lem took turns holding the basket.

One Saturday while I was cleaning the feeding trough for the nestlings, I heard a short, startled scream coming from one of the adult pens. Within seconds, I ran to the pen and peeped through the wire fence. Linda was standing with both arms around the egg basket while Lem was bending forward, waving his right hand, and slowly maneuvering his left hand toward the ground. It was a move I had seen him do many times to catch snakes. With a sudden swoop of his left hand, he grabbed a four-foot Eastern king snake. Holding the snake firmly behind its head, Lem held it up for her to see. She took a step backward.

"It's just a king snake. Not poisonous," he said.

"What's it doing in here?"

"Having lunch. Every day grains of duck feed drop into the straw attractin' field mice. King snakes love to eat field mice."

"Are there any other kind of snakes?"

"Yes, unfortunately, the mice also attract copperheads and we have to watch out for them too."

"Lem!" she said with a whip in her voice, "you waited all this time before telling me that?"

"It's okay, Linda, they're afraid of people. They can hear and smell us comin', so they slip away and hide. As you can see, king snakes are black with white stripes and they stand out against the light-colored straw, but copperheads are brownish with a light pattern on their backs. They blend in with the straw, and they like to slide under it and hide until we leave."

"Unless we step on one, right?"

"Well…yes, you don't want to do that. It doesn't happen often. How many times have you been in these pens, and have you ever seen or stepped on a snake?" he asked.

"You know I haven't. Have *you* ever stepped on one?"

"Actually…yes."

"Did he bite you?"

"He snapped at me, but he missed."

"And what did you do with him?"

"He got away."

"Really?" she said as she looked at the hay around her.

"My dad told me never to be afraid of the snakes you can see, like this big black beauty here. The ones to fear are the snakes you can't see, that are hidden, out of sight, invisible, like our copperheads."

"You're not making me feel any better," she said as she looked all around her feet again.

"I'm sure you're safe. You seldom see copperheads when king snakes are around because, in addition to eatin' rodents, king snakes like to eat other snakes includin' copperheads. That's why they're called *king snakes.*"

"How do you get rid of them?"

"Well, the copperheads have to be caught, then killed. We can't put poison out because of the ducks. The king snakes, even though they eat other snakes, have to be exterminated because they also love to eat the little ducklings and eggs."

"Eggs? How do they do that?"

"They swallow them whole."

"So how do you get rid of them?"

"You've probably seen a few golf balls in the nests, right?"

"Yes, I thought they were there to inspire the laying ducks or something like that."

"No, ducks don't need any inspiration to lay. The king snakes think golf balls are eggs, and swallow the balls, and can't digest them."

"That's cruel."

"Yep."

Satisfied that he had properly consoled her, Lem left the pen to get rid of the snake while Linda remained in place clutching the egg basket and watching her feet.

I let Lem walk away before speaking to Linda. "He's right," I said as I entered the pen, "In all my years I've only seen a handful of copperheads slinking around. Sometimes I see the straw moving like something's sliding underneath the surface, and I like to think the snakes are busy, secretly getting rid of the mice."

"That's still not very comforting," she said.

"I'm sorry," I said as I patted her back. We walked back to the house. Bearcat jumped around like we had been gone a week instead of an hour. We sat at the kitchen table writing the date on each egg. The dog stretched out on the floor between us. We put all the eggs into a warming cabinet where they would stay for five days, then they would be tested to see if they should go to incubation or to market.

I didn't know how much Lem shared personal things with Linda, and I hesitated to bring it up, but Lem had not mentioned my job at all since he visited me at the bookstore. I knew he must have imagined things about me and my work that weren't true, and if he discussed it with Linda, then I needed her advice about what he was thinking.

"Have you noticed that Lem has been more quiet than usual lately?" I said.

"Well, he's been a little moody, but it's okay, I get that way sometimes."

"Did he mentioned that he had met some of my friends at work?"

Linda put her pen down and thought for a minute, then said, "Yes, I understand now why you think he has been quiet. He's a brooder. You know it takes him a long time to say what's on his mind, but he has to chew on it for a while first then spit it out. I'm sure you know what I'm talking about."

"I want to know if he has shared his feelings with you about my job and my association with certain people," said Trish.

"Communists?"

"Yes."

"He kept it to himself at first. I knew there was something bugging him, and I let him stew until he was ready. It was a little over two weeks ago when he went to Chapel Hill. It took a little while before he let it all come gushing out."

"What happened?"

"It came out first in the color of his face and then he was almost in tears. In all the years I've known him, I never saw him cry, not even when your dad and momma died, but he came as close to it as I have ever seen. He ended up in my arms out there on the porch, and I had to be a mother to him until it all drained out. We spent the night on the couch. Afterward, he returned to his usual calm, quiet self."

"Yes, I remember seeing you asleep on the couch as I went out to work. Does he hate me for what I'm doing?"

"Oh God, no. He loves you and fears he's losing you."

"But why? All I'm doing is kind of like charity work. I don't bother him with it or even talk about it."

"Trish, he doesn't think what you are doing is good, and he will *never* believe that you are actually helping people. He didn't tell me any details about what you do, but I know that's how he feels."

"He doesn't *know* any details about what I do, because I've never told him."

"Let me put it another way. He doesn't think it will end well for you and it worries him sick."

"I have to keep working, but I still need him. I still need to be close to him. I left the farm to work somewhere else, and I don't think he'll ever get over it."

"I don't know if he's going to change. If he tells me more, I'll let you know. All I can say now is be *patient*."

Linda and I could talk for hours about anything, but our favorite subject was always Lem. Not many people understood my big brother. They thought of him as a big feral cat that was almost, but not quite, tamed.

I finally brought up the question I had been wanting to ask for a couple of years. "You two ever think about marriage?"

"Yes," she answered to my surprise.

"And what did you two decide?"

"Well, I'm sure we both have thought about it, but we haven't exactly discussed it yet."

"Why not?"

"I don't know. We just haven't gotten around to it yet."

"Sorry for being nosy. It's just…you know Lem and I were always so close and everything."

"Oh, yes. It's okay."

Linda had known Lem since they were four years old,

and she was the only person who had known him longer than me, and maybe the only person outside of the family that was never intimidated by him. In spite of his size, he was never a bully. I never thought of him as a *feral cat*, but more like a big watermelon, the largest of all fruit with a thick, dark, solid skin completely concealing and protecting its soft and sweet interior.

"I told you I'm going to be honest," said Linda. "I wish you weren't doing it—working with those people."

"You mean the communists?"

"Yes, of course!"

"To tell you the truth, sometimes I get scared, really scared, over-my-head scared, but other times I'm just so happy that I'm doing something besides raising ducks."

"I thought you love the ducks."

"I *do*, of course, I do, but this is really *Lem's* farm, and if you two get married, this will be *your* house and *your* farm, and I'll be so happy for you. When that happens, and when I come here, I'll be a guest. So sooner or later, I won't have a home and I still won't have a real job. I probably won't have any real, permanent friends."

"Trish, you know you can't work for the Communist Party the rest of your life!"

"I know."

•••

Animals, especially dogs, always know when someone around them is sad or in pain. Bearcat stayed close by me that night. I let him sleep on the oval rug in my room, which was a real treat. When I woke early the next morning, he was sitting at the bottom of the bed looking at me, like a guard on duty.

# CHAPTER FOURTEEN

## TRISH
## JULY 1947

Will left a note saying he wanted to meet me after the store closed. At five o'clock sharp, I held the door for the last customer to leave before I locked up. I straightened the displays on the counter while waiting for Will to invite me back. Will frequently lost himself in his work, so I went back to see how he was doing and if he was ready to talk. I hadn't taken more than three steps into the cluttered room when I discovered Will with his arms wrapped around Cynthia Lewis. Without making a sound, I turned to leave. She breathed in deeply then let out deep sobs. That's when I saw Will's left hand patting her back just above the shoulder blade, while his right hand lightly patted the back of her hair, the way a father would comfort his teenage daughter. He said something softly about her pain and something about sticking it out. Without a sound, I slipped back into the store until I heard Cynthia leave through the back door.

"Come on back," Will said when he saw me peek into the room.

"I didn't want to disturb you."

"No, I'm sorry to make you wait."

"What happened to Cynthia?" I said.

"Very sad." He said quietly. "Her roommate moved out, and almost all the friends she had made here, turned on her."

"Oh, my God. What happened?"

"Her roomy found her literature bag under the bed."

"What's the matter with that?"

"It was her c-communist literature, and Cynthia was forced to tell about being a member of the Party."

"And all of her friends left her?"

"Yes, they all turned on her, except for friends in the Party."

"But why did she keep a bag of communist literature like that in her dorm room? Why not just keep it here with all the other stuff?"

"Good question. I only know that Francis gave her the bag, and told her to keep it safe, in her room."

"Was it a big bag?"

"It was a big c-canvas bag full of books and pamphlets — very heavy."

"How did Francis expect her to keep something like that a secret in the dorm?"

"I don't know. I can't figure out what he's thinking half the time."

"I have to confess… I walked back here earlier and saw her leaning against you. I've never heard anybody her age cry like that."

"Unfortunately, I've s-seen it a lot. There's no way for me to prepare young people in our flock for what it t-takes to do this work. I coach them to be very careful who they share it with, but still, I've spent a lot of time, picking them off the floor, p-patching up their souls the best I can, and getting them back to work for the cause, but sooner or later it happens to many of us. Some people go through it several times and still bounce back, but some just disappear."

"What can I do for Cynthia? Maybe I can take her home with me for a weekend or something."

"I would love to think she's stronger than she looked a little while ago. But like I said, I've seen it many times. If she can't stand up to the pressure of being different and thinking differently from almost everybody else, I'm told she has to go. I'm supposed to forget about her and replace her and believe me, Trish, that's very hard on me. Understanding why we have to go through that is as difficult as d-doing it.

"I just wish there was something I could do for her."

"I'm sorry you saw Cynthia that way, but believe it or not, this is one of the things I wanted to talk to you about today."

"I'm not even a member of the Party, so I don't think you're going to have to pick *me* off the floor."

"Hope not. You've been a very helpful worker for us, but if you stay, you *will* lose your friends because of your association with us, and it *will* hurt. I think you'll get over it, though, because I know you're strong, and you appreciate what we're doing. I want to warn you that the more of this work you do, the more isolated you will become. It's as simple as that."

"How about you?" I asked, "Did you ever lose your friends when you first joined the Party?"

"No, it was easy for me. I never really had that many friends, and my family gave up on me a long t-time ago." He pulled two mugs out of a drawer and said, "Got hot coffee in the other room. Let me get you some, and you can pull the other chair over here near my desk so we can talk some more."

I had lots of questions that morning, and the more he talked, the more questions I had. I didn't know where to start. The coffeepot he placed on the desk was filled to the top. I was afraid he expected us to talk all night. He sat on his old swivel chair and poured two cups full of jet-black coffee.

"Cream?" he asked.

"Yes, please, *lots* of it."

"Sugar?"

"Yes, two."

"I thought it would be good to t-talk about the events at the Hillsboro Mill, and what they mean," he said.

"Well good, 'cause I need to hear something about it. I definitely enjoyed meeting Betty—what an interesting person and sweet family. She was on my mind all week, and she seemed so interested in things you told her, but, what was that all about back there with the police and everything? How often does that stuff happen?"

Will sat with his elbow draped over the arm of his chair, and his cup clenched in his left forefinger. I paused for a moment as he took his first sip of coffee. It was a long sip, and he shuddered slightly before saying, "Y-you do like to jump right in there, don't you?"

"Everything was crazy when we left the mill. Of *course*, I want to jump right in."

"Trish, let me start by explaining more about what I do and why."

"Okay, that would be good."

"I think we have something in common."

"Yes, I guess so."

"A few years ago, I joined several groups that accomplished lots of things and won battles for all kinds of people."

"What groups?"

"You know we've t-talked about the CPUSA, the National Party."

He paused and watched my face — then I replied, "Yes, and you said I would hear bad things about it. Well, you were right."

"The Party started about three decades ago, and some of our members were a little overanxious to make the kind of changes this country needs — changes to the way our society and our government treat people."

"What kind of changes?"

"Changing the kind of things Betty was talking about. In the early days, the Party didn't know how to control the v-violent opposition they ran into, so they approached the problem with their *own* violence. Believe me, I don't want violence any more than you do."

"That day at the mill ended in violence, and I don't want any part of it," I said.

"I know, but you need to understand that our work there hasn't ended. Because of what we started, many of those people who are getting paid practically nothing for their honest work, are already calling us for help, and they want to meet soon."

"Like Betty?"

"Yes, she's one of them, and sh-she's already asked her pastor to let us meet at their church."

"But why can't we get it all done without knocking heads with everybody?"

"We can most of the time. Trish, if you're g-going to help these people, you can't worry too much about *how* we get it done.

"So what you're saying is that *sometimes* there will be fighting, right?"

"Yes, but not usually. Trish, the phones are ringing, and we're moving forward. That's all that matters."

He stopped for another long sip of coffee, then waited for me to reply. I didn't know what to say. Will was such a gentle, soft-spoken man that, I couldn't imagine him fighting or encouraging anyone else into violence. He carefully watched my face to see if anything he said was upsetting me, and whenever he thought it was, he started over with softer language or a new subject. Every now and then, he gave me a reassuring smile.

"Okay, then who are you in the Party? I mean what's your position?"

"I'm Vice Chairman of the NCCP, and I answer to the Chairman, Francis. He answers to a complex group at the national level, the CPUSA in New York. They also have a chairman as the prime leader over all branches in the country."

"Is the chairman Russian or something like that?

"No, but the Russian Communist Party inspired and orchestrated the CPUSA decades ago and they still make demands on us."

"And you obey?"

"I do what the CPUSA says. My current connection with the Soviets is limited, but I have great respect for what they've accomplished worldwide. Nobody has changed the world more than Lenin and Stalin. Some of the Soviet demands make their way through the organization and all the way down to Francis, and then me."

"And you do what Francis says?"

"Do you have a problem with Francis?"

"Oh...Well, he's very...determined and... kind of different."

"Different?"

"Well, I've never heard an accent like that."

"He's from *Jersey*."

"You mean *New Jersey*, right?"

"Yes, of course."

"To tell you the truth, when I'm alone with him, he makes me nervous," I said.

"Why?"

"It's hard to pin down, but...let me put it this way, I'm not surprised that he was one of the men that got into a fight at the mill."

"We want our movement to be a peaceful transition, believe me. It's complex, very complex. We're all over the country, in every state. The thing you've got to understand is that every part of the movement must work together as one big machine, and people like me and you can't see the whole picture."

"Okay, what's the *whole picture*? What's the *goal*?"

"The worldwide goal is to enlighten every country into an understanding of what it means to have uniform equality—a kind of society they've never dreamed possible. But it will eventually require everybody to be on board."

"*Everybody*?"

"Yes."

"How?"

"In stages. Karl Marx said that before any nation is

ready to accept *c-communism,* they first must embrace *socialism."*

"Aren't they different things?"

"Every true communist will tell you that the only difference between socialism and communism is: *socialism is the beautiful promising bud,* and *communism is the full flower."*

I pulled my wood chair closer to him, and said, "Now, would you please tell me exactly how you got into this?"

Will put his mug down, planted his forearms across his knees, and stared over his clutched hands for a few moments, then said, "I grew up not far from here. My family was wealthy, but they had what I call, *a poverty of compassion."*

"What's that?"

"A blind eye to the way people all around us were being treated. *That* drove me mad. My parents had no interest in the welfare of the c-community. No interest in improving the pitiful plight of the Negro population. They were proud to be rank *capitalists,* and I discovered I was a hopeless *socialist.* By the time I was in my teens, my family couldn't stand to be with me or talk to me. My only communication with them today is a monthly payment from a trust fund Dad set up to keep me independent, and away from him. When I first came here, my course of study, along with my life, had *no purpose.* No place to go, and no place to return. I contemplated killing myself."

I couldn't hold back a loud, full-throated gasp—so loud it actually startled him for a moment. "But *why?*" I asked.

Will closed his eyes and sat still for a long time. He shook a little as if he were trying to pull his mind through a jumble of conflicting thoughts. He finally replied, "Like I said, it was all hopeless, because the world had evolved into some k-kind of giant mechanism, driving against all the things and all the people I believed in. And who was I, but a scrawny bookworm lost in the middle of a big university? I had something to say, but no voice."

His chin quivered as he sat straight up and continued, "That's when I met a group of young students and graduate student instructors who enjoyed friendly debates right here at the bookstore. I st-started attending, and two of them encouraged me to join the SCA, Student Communist Association. I did, and eventually, I became a member of the CPUSA, and the NCCP and nothing has been the same since."

"So it's a kind of rebirth?"

"Yes, in a way. I'm sure I owe my life to it, and I would sacrifice *everything* for it."

"Sounds like a religious experience. Did you ever believe in God?"

"When I was young I did, but I haven't pursued it. Communism can't tolerate any other power but itself. Communism and God can't live together—matter is the sum total of the universe; there is no such thing as spirit. But I do believe in a kind of savior."

"Okay, who?"

"Actually, it's not a single person; it's the intelligent c-class of people—those of us who are the true thinkers, who have a moral responsibility to help the less fortunate— no matter what it costs, and no matter what we have to do to make it happen."

"Are you part of the intelligent class?"

"Yes, I believe that I am."

"When you say you have a responsibility to help the less fortunate, no matter what, does that include using violence?"

"The answer from me is *no, if at all possible.*"

"What's the Party's answer?" I asked.

"The Party's answer is, *whatever it takes, including violence.*"

"And what about Francis?"

"Francis...Francis is in step with the Party."

"Which means what?"

"Which means, he would eagerly support doing whatever it takes, including violence," he said.

"And *he* is the number-one communist in the Carolinas?"

"Yes, and now NCCP is growing beyond the Carolinas, and I'm number two."

"When are you going to be the number-one?"

"Pretty damn soon," he said with a perfectly straight face and no emotion. That was the first hint he gave me of competition at the top.

"I notice you and Francis keep totally separate agendas."

"That's right. We do different things. As an example, I joined the Progressive Party, to work on the Henry Wallace campaign for President. Francis supports him but did not join. He left all that to me."

"Is that the Wallace that was Vice President to Roosevelt?"

"Yes, but he has a much more aggressive, progressive agenda than FDR, and everybody's going to love him."

"I'm sorry I don't know anything about him," I said.

"He's giving a speech in Raleigh soon. Maybe you'd

like to attend."

"I suppose so." I didn't know anything about him, but Will must have thought it would be helpful for me to hear him speak."

"You could learn lots from him," said Will. "You have a lot to learn, you know? But I believe you will eventually do important things for the Party."

"Will …." I placed my hand on the side of my cheek and closed my eyes. "We, my family, just work our farm. We never had much influence beyond ourselves. I've never pictured myself that way—you know, a courageous person achieving things, and all that stuff."

"This will surprise you, but you're already in the middle of something important right now."

"Me? I don't think so!"

Will clasped his hands, shook them slightly, and said, "Okay, two things to remember… Karl Marx said *no s-social revolution is p-possible without women deeply involved,* and FDR said that *the nation's number- one economic p-problem is the Southern economy.*"

"What does *that* mean?"

"You, like everybody else in this state, underestimate the importance of what's going on here. The textile industry in North Carolina is the envy of the world, but the wages being paid are *p-pathetic,* so we're working to strengthen wages. After we've accomplished that, it's a proven fact that productivity will n-naturally increase because of more motivated workers; therefore, profit will increase. So as the value of labor increases, because they are making more money for the company, the workers can legitimately demand their share of the company's profits. St-Starting here in the Carolinas, the wealth will spread.

And the *Nation's number-one economic problem*, as FDR called it, will be solved. You and I, with our friends, can help do that, and it would become a *model* for the country."

"Oh, God!" I said in a whisper. "Will, I don't think I can...or *want* to understand all this."

"I know it all sounds so different and foreign, but tell me what you saw in Betty's face?"

"I saw a young, pretty woman with three children, no husband, a lousy job, and a willingness to reach out for whatever's going to pull her out of the mud."

Will stared at me, and nodded for a moment, then said very deliberately, "You and I, and the p-party are going to do that for her."

"You didn't hear what I told you!" Then I repeated slowly, "I'm a farmer's daughter, and I grew up on a *duck* farm. I've never been out of North Carolina, and *shoot*, I've barely been out of these three counties. I've never thought about capitalism, or textile worker problems, or socialism, or any stuff like that."

"I know, but, I can s-see you are a fast learner."

I wasn't sure I understood what he meant, but I nodded, then returned the chair to the wall and went back to the store. The uncomfortable feeling whirling in my head couldn't find a resting place. It was all too new.

A separate bookcase between two stuffed chairs had a sign on it labeled, "GOVERNMENT AND NEW THOUGHT." Two small books were written by Will. One of them is the book he gave me when I first started working there. I had already read most of it. I understood what he was saying, but couldn't see how it applied to us. I started reading the second book during my morning and afternoon breaks, and during most of my lunch hour. I liked the sound of the goal they called "peaceful coexistence". I liked the idea of elimination of poverty, racial equality, and the relationship between collective and personal security, but their arguments about social reform, revolution, fascism, capitalism, communism, civil disobedience, and governmental overthrow still frightened me so much I wanted to run somewhere and hide. In my mind, I was fighting a changing picture of myself. I wasn't sure if I was fighting who I thought I had been, or who Will wanted me to be. Maybe I was fighting for my life.

A couple of the books had pictures of mill workers, who looked just like the ones we talked to in Hillsboro, especially the ones with blank faces stripped of emotion as if finding a better life was a forgotten fantasy. I thought about Betty, and how her children came to the car and looked at us like we were Santa Clauses arriving in a big black Plymouth. I thought about Will, and how he had opened my mind so quickly. I wished that someday I could be half as smart as he was. I loved thinking of myself as a student—still learning, just like those across the street walking to their classes every day. As long as I pictured myself that way, I didn't think I had to make any decisions or form any opinions. I just needed to trust that someday I would understand it all.

Jack Hemphill

# CHAPTER FIFTEEN

## WILL
## AUGUST 1947

I knew it was Francis the moment I heard him bang the heel of his fist on my door three times. He had spent the last few months at headquarters in New York.

"I bet you thought you'd never see me again," said Francis as he walked into my apartment.

"That never crossed my m-mind."

"Will, you are the worse liar I ever knew."

"Okay, we all thought you'd be back about now."

"So what have I missed?"

"Things have happened. We now have four Party members b-buried in the labor force at Reynolds Tobacco plant—three line workers and one in lower management."

"And how's it going?" he asked.

"Everybody's still throwing punches, but we've got a lot of br-brave workers. There's a meeting tomorrow night between union and management. You want to go?"

"Maybe you should continue working that one," he said.

"*You* should be there, I said." I was surprised he didn't jump on the chance to get back into the largest union project we had ever attempted to pull off—a project he started and nurtured for years.

"If I go, I'll take Trish," I said.

"Why?"

"Give her more exposure."

"You think she's ready for that level of conflict."

"I d-don't know."

Francis said, "She's not even a party member yet. Let her get through the Hillsboro Mill project first. If she's still standing—if she's still with us—then you can talk about showing her more."

"You're right, she's got a lot to learn, but she's very bright. The truth is she's m-more than smart, although I've been careful not to push her. Francis, I think she can be good for us."

"It doesn't matter. I have ways to use her however she turns out. We'll see, but don't get attached. Sometimes I think she's *too* smart, and at the same time, *too* innocent. As far as I know, she could be the perfect FBI mole running around under our nose."

"*Mole?* That's ridiculous! She's not quite nineteen years old. Why would you say that?"

"Before I came here today, I went by the bookstore. There was a man standing beside our shelf, the one with all the Party literature. He was talking to Trish."

"What's the matter with that? Talking to customers is part of her job."

"I recognized the man. He's got a face you can't forget," I said.

"Who was he?"

"He's an FBI agent, and he's been working for years to uncover and expose Party activity."

"How do you know that?"

"Because, a couple of years ago, he pulled me aside at a rally, flashed his badge, and said he was Agent Greenwood, and then questioned me about what I was doing there."

"What did you t-tell him?"

"Of course, I lied. Told him I was just a spectator."

"Did he recognize you today?"

"He didn't see me, but I know it's him, and he spent a lot of time with Trish. So my question still is, are you *sure* you can trust her, Will?"

"I am."

"But *why*?

"Because I think she's incapable of lying to us, and she's naturally friendly, and always happy to talk to strangers."

"Hope you're right, but if you're not, we'll have to get rid of her, and find another girl."

"That's not the big problem here. If an FBI agent has been in our store, standing beside our literature, and q-questioning people, he's going to keep coming back as long as he thinks he's getting information. So what do we do to stop him?"

"We can't. We just gotta watch him, and we should start hiding our files.

"How are we going to do that?"

"You'll find a way. First of all, don't tell the rest of the staff about the agent. No need to frighten them. Anyway, they've all been told how to talk about communism to strangers, and they know not to discuss specifics about any of our activities."

"I think Trish should know we're being watched."

"No, let her stay ignorant!"

I could see that Francis was agitated. I'm certain Trish

needed my advice, but I just let it drop. Arguing with him had always been as fruitless as yelling under water.

I changed the subject, "We're still growing. We now have a communist on the UNC teaching staff."

"Who?"

"Hans Freistadt, who joined the UNC Physics Department on a teaching fellowship."

"Great, what else?"

"We've also increased membership in the Communist Student Club."

'How many?"

"We are up to thirty-five from both UNC and Duke including a professor from each university. The students in the club are majoring in English, French, economics, history, math, literature, journalism, geography, dramatic art, psychology, physical education, law, sociology, and anthropology. Also, we started a separate club for Negros, with six members, and all of them work for or near UNC.

"What's the reaction to this communist invasion?"

"The Daily Tarheel is going nuts, but the administration is urging tolerance and requesting that all    students stay focused on studies and not protest."

"I don't care if they go nuts."

"I see but there's more resistance to us now, more than I've ever s-seen. That agent in our bookstore is a good example. The FBI is still trying to infiltrate us and get inside some of the unions we are working with, especially the Reynolds Union."

"Don't worry about it."

"Okay…but an FBI agent could walk through that…d-door right now, that door you just banged on, and arrest us."

"I know that, but don't be stupid. They passed the Smith Act seven years ago, and here we are still at work and still secretly planting our seeds everywhere. They'll never see it coming, not now, maybe not ten years from now. Maybe twenty years and beyond they'll begin to see it."

Jack Hemphill

# CHAPTER SIXTEEN

## TRISH
## SEPTEMBER 1947

Will may not have been the most articulate man, but he was extremely organized, and he laid out work for all of the thirty-five or forty men and women in our group. We had a big weekend planned, starting with a meeting in the backyard of the Hillsboro ARP Church. Every worker in the mill was invited.

At five-thirty on a Friday afternoon, ten cars were lined up behind the bookstore. I sat in the front seat beside Will. Carole sat in the back with a man named Tim Horn, who was new to our group and was a graduate student transferring from Wake Forest. He was a nice-looking man, not married, pleasant, and apparently already had plenty of experience with the Party. He knew exactly what to do when we got to the church, even though he had not yet attended any of Will's training sessions.

Francis drove the lead car and we were second. Eight other cars followed us in caravan style to the Church. Gill Holstrum drove the last car. I felt like I was part of an army. When we arrived, most of the plant workers were already there walking around, talking with each other, and shaking hands, but they all stood still and watched us as our procession came to a stop and we exited our cars at the same time. Francis led the troops down the hill to the meeting. The first person I saw was Betty, who came out of the crowd and hugged me and thanked me for coming. Will introduced her to Tim and the four of us stayed together the whole night.

Francis instantly became the center of attention and turned into a flaming crusader, preaching for fair pay and employment security for everyone. The crowd sat on chairs borrowed from the Sunday School. Some sat on the ground. They immediately fell under Francis's irresistible spell of hope, destiny, and the power of a righteous cause. Every fifteen minutes, he stopped and we sang old gospel hymns that everybody knew. Tim, Will, Betty, and I swayed in rhythm together. Francis's high-pitched voice floated on the cool twilight air. His message was given with such authority and unwavering strength, that it sounded like it came directly from Michael, the Archangel. After the sunset, the only light we had, came from two dim lamps on the rear of the church directly behind Francis. In the soft glow, the groups of people around us melted into silhouettes of heads and shoulders, arms and hands, fused together into a single form. By eight o'clock Francis gave a signal, and we handed out the leaflets and answered questions as we were trained to do. We then returned to our cars, but Francis stood in front of his car looking down the hill. Someone in the back seat of Will's car said, "Holstrum's still down there!" I rolled my window down and saw him with three of his crew talking to a small gathering under a clump of trees. After another minute, Francis got into the car and slammed the door. We all knew Holstrum would, sooner or later, pay a penalty for his independence.

As we drove away, I saw Betty disappear back into the crowd. I had known her for about a year. I had never seen the look of expectation on her face like I saw that night. All I thought about that night, and for days after, was that I would do all I could to keep her hope from being in vain.

Jack Hemphill

# CHAPTER SEVENTEEN

## TRISH
## OCTOBER 1947

I was nervous as I drove to Raleigh. About a mile outside of the city, I saw buildings peeking over the treetops. Henry Wallace was speaking that night as part of his presidential campaign tour for the Progressive Party. I never thought I would ever have an opportunity to hear a speech by a former U.S. Vice President. Carole had been given instructions to meet me in front of Memorial Auditorium an hour and a half before the speech was to start. I had never even seen the auditorium before, although some of my friends from high school had gone to concerts and North Carolina State basketball games in the building. One of my friends had attended a Democratic Convention there.

As instructed, I entered Raleigh on Hillsborough Street, turned right on Dawson, and then immediately left on East South Street. In front of me stood the massive stone building with six columns at least twenty-five feet high towering over granite steps and five pairs of double doors. The building took up the entire block, and I circled it twice to get a good look all around. Each side was equally impressive, and people were walking toward it from all directions. On Dawson Street and South Street, lines of picketers holding posters fixed to long wood sticks marched up and down the sidewalks protesting Wallace's progressive policies.

Even though there was a parking lot behind the building and one across the street from the front entrance, I decided to drive another two blocks further east and park under a street lamp. The sun was already setting. From the back seat, I grabbed some of the pamphlets Will printed for Carole and me to hand out that night. To avoid the protesters, I walked on the far side of the street and crossed in mid-block directly in front of the main entrances. I looked for Carole around each side of the building but couldn't find her.

Wide-eyed young men were dashing down the walks, older men in suits and ties were marching toward the building, women wearing smart hats with feathers were climbing the granite stairs, and several groups of Negro men were walking through the front doors and looking up at the columns towering two stories above them. I opened the box of flyers and pulled out a dozen or so. The box of pamphlets had been handed to me only a few minutes before I left the bookstore, and I had not read them. So, I took a quick moment to scan the printed message which appeared to be Mr. Wallace's basic policies. I walked to the side of the building, far from the protesters, and started giving out pamphlets. Some people took them and smiled, some just ignored me, but within an hour I had given out the entire box of papers. I still had a half hour before the event was to start, so I headed toward my car to get the second box. A husky man carrying a poster nailed to a wood stick approached me. I didn't look at him and tried to walk past him, but he leaned toward me and yelled, "Are you the one handing out this junk?" He held one of our flyers in the air.

"Excuse me?" I said.

"Is this your garbage?" he said waving the paper at me.

"Why do you want to know," I asked, simply to avoid answering his question.

"Because it's communist crap!"

"What makes you think that?"

"It says who it's from across the bottom of the page. Are *you* a *communist*?"

"No!" I said. When I looked over the paper, an hour earlier, I had completely missed the note at the bottom of the front page saying, *printed by NCCP*.

The man hesitated a moment, then said, "You better find out who you're working for and wake up — or better still, why don't you save yourself the pain and just go home!"

I stomped around him, crossed South Street, and went back to my car. By then the street lights had turned on. I grabbed the second box of flyers and returned to the auditorium. I only had ten minutes left before the speech was to start, and I hurried through the big doors into the building. The nervousness I felt in my stomach all day rose to my head. My pulse was pounded like a drum. The front lobby stretched across the full width of the building. The floors were made of some kind of light-colored stone that matched the walls. I entered the auditorium and found a seat at the back as close to the door as I could. Before that day, the largest crowd I had ever seen was about two hundred people at a Chatham County High

School football game. Just being in that auditorium was frightening enough, but it took me ten minutes to take in the size of the crowd around me. Three thousand people turned out that night to hear Mr. Wallace. There must have been a thousand individual chairs placed in careful rows in front of me on the main floor, and fixed seating wrapped around the entire auditorium forming a giant bowl. A platform sat at the far end of the floor where a dozen dignified men and women were seated waiting for the event to start.

After an introduction of some important people, Mr. Wallace took the stage. The applause was more than generous, and he seemed surprised. He was a good-looking man with a full head of slightly graying hair. I sat a long way from him, but even from there, I thought he looked a lot like Jimmy Stewart. Will asked me to take notes on the highlights of his speech, and I jotted them down in my small notebook.

Most of the spectators were heavy supporters of Wallace. Some people were there because they opposed him, and some were just curious. The audience was about sixty percent men. Mr. Wallace was an impressive speaker, and he spoke slowly and clearly. Some of his statements caused most of the crowd to jump to their feet and applaud. Some of his thoughts brought a response mostly from women. Other remarks caused loud cheers from the men. He talked at length about racial equality, and the Negro groups applauded respectfully but did not stand or yell out. When he said he would find a way to offer free college education to *all* Americans, the young people in the crowd stood and cheered like they were at a basketball game. The older men stood and clapped when he guaranteed that every family had the right to a decent home at a price *all* could afford. He received a mild, but polite applause after his statement that he would take the largest banks, the railroads, the electric power, and gas and place them all under public ownership. Late in his speech, he denounced the current anti-Soviet *hysteria* in the United States as baseless, and he condemned Truman's loyalty program.

His last statement received the loudest and longest applause. I wrote it down as fast as I could, trying to get it exactly right. Mr. Wallace said, "The Progressive Party believes that enduring peace among peoples of the world community is possible only through *world law* enacted by a *world federal legislature* with powers to safeguard the defense and welfare of all mankind."

Twice protesters sitting in the higher rows along both sides of the auditorium broke out in anti-Wallace chants. Wallace stopped both times to let them finish, settle down, and when they were quiet, he continued his speech.

He talked for over an hour, and when he was finished, he turned a full circle waiving to the crowd on all sides of the auditorium. After he finally sat down, the applause continued for five more minutes.

It was hard not to be impressed with a man who spoke so well, looked like Jimmy Stewart, and promised so much. I *wanted* it to be true. I wanted all the things he was proposing to be possible, even though I had no idea how it could happen. I felt a rush of joy bubbling in me, and I wanted to hold on to that feeling.

I stood and tucked the box of flyers under my arm. Loud voices from protesters exploded from the tiered seating above me to my right. Some Wallace supporters screamed back at the demonstrators. Other supporters around the room started chanting Wallace's name.

Since I was so close to the door I scooted out with others that were hoping to get away quickly. In spite of the conflict at the end, the crowd was almost giddy over the speech, and they eagerly took my handouts. After fifteen minutes, I had only about a dozen sheets left.

As I walked down South Street, someone yelled at me, "You don't listen do you girl?" I looked up and saw the hefty protester who accosted me before the speech. Beside him were two other men carrying signs on long wooden sticks. He reached out his hand toward my box of flyers. I pulled it close to my chest and he said, "Give me that garbage!" I took a few quick steps backward. They ran toward me, but suddenly stopped, turned away, and scampered down the sidewalk out of sight.

Several people were watching. I heard a man's voice behind me saying, "Miss Basil, are you alright?" I was afraid to look, so I waited for the man to walk in front of me.

"Are you alright?" he asked me again.

"Yes, no problem, but...thanks." He looked familiar, but I couldn't remember from where.

He reached into his breast pocket, pulled out a badge, and said, "I met you in the bookstore. I didn't identify myself then, but I'm FBI Agent Greenwood."

"Oh, yes, I remember you. What are you doing here?" I knew that was a stupid question as soon as I said it. He gave me a blank stare for a moment, before saying, "I was assigned to be at this speech."

"So, what were you looking for?" I closed my eyes afraid I had asked another mindless question.

"We knew there would be protesters here tonight, and possibly some communists. I've already spoken to the protesters," he said.

"Oh really?" I didn't dare say more. He put his badge away, pulled out a copy of my flyers, and held it high for a moment, then said, "I'm glad you didn't give him the box, but now you have to give it to me."

Without a word, I handed over the near empty box and waited for him to speak."

"Where are you parked, Miss Basil?"

"Two blocks down the street, under the light."

"Why don't I walk you down there?" He made it clear I had no choice, but I was glad he was going to escort me.

The two blocks seemed like ten, however it gave me time to think. "Thank you for scaring those guys away and walking me back here," I said. He obviously knew all about me and about what was going on at the bookstore. I just wanted to get out of there and get home as soon as possible.

"Drive carefully, Miss Basil," is all he said. In my mirror, I saw him watching me until I drove out of sight.

The following day at the bookstore, Carole explained that she had driven to the auditorium, but because of the protesters, she turned around and went home. She said she expected that I would do the same thing.

Wallace's southern tour continued for the rest of the year. His supporters became more enthusiastic with each speech, and the opposition became angrier.

# CHAPTER EIGHTEEN

## TRISH
## MARCH 1948

Will bought a Carolina blue 1948 Plymouth. I couldn't remember being in anything so luxurious in my life. I guess the closest thing to it was the auditorium in downtown Raleigh. When I rode with him, I felt so fine and rich that it was a little embarrassing to visit the people we were helping — the people in little houses, clustered in mill towns scattered around poor sections of Greensboro, Hillsboro, and Durham. Betty's house was on the top of a hill with a view that looked over dozens of brown roofs, cascading away like so many toadstools on the side of a gully, waiting for the next rain to wash them away.

Betty's children spotted Will's bright-blue car the moment it entered the neighborhood, and Christine came running to give me a hug and do silly things to make me laugh.

"Oh, how you've grown!" I said. It had been over a year since I had seen her.

"You still think I'm pretty?" she asked.

"Prettier than ever."

I was so proud of Betty. I thought she might be too shy to help us organize her fellow workers and convince them how much better off they could be. Six months earlier, with my help, she wrote a petition of basic concerns, got it signed by all the workers, and delivered it to the president of the mill. The mill's response was an informal note posted on the two employee bulletin boards. The note said that they would continue improving wages and working conditions to the best of the company's abilities. The note went on to say that they appreciate the loyalty so many of the employees had shown over the years. Of course, they ignored most of the basic concerns in the petition.

We had spent the winter and spring helping Betty and her friends prepare a formal threat to strike unless certain grievances were met. All workers showed uniform determination without a single doubt about what they were doing. Betty had not written many of the grievances down, but she was able to quote them to Will, who jotted them in his notebook.

"Well," Betty said, "The top items are money and more holidays, not jus' Christmas, but Thanksgiving and maybe Good Friday before Easter."

"Of course, those are reasonable requests," I said as Will wrote it down.

"Also," she continued, "Those of us, who are *winders*, get our salary docked when the thread on the bobbin breaks, and we get behind in production, but it's not our fault when the thread breaks. It just snaps sometimes and we can't afford to have our pay cut."

"Okay, good. What's next?" said Will as he scribbled in his notebook.

"Also, in the summertime, it gets so hot. I jus' 'bout pas out. The shift foreman comes 'round and opens the high windows to get a breeze through, but it's not nearly enough. And the yarn has to be baked in the steam chamber, and anybody that has to work anywhere near it will tell you that when the steam chamber is goin', it gets up to one hundred degrees most of the day. We know that 'cause there's a thermometer on the wall outside the chamber. They need to do somethin' 'bout that."

"Good, Betty. Anything else?" Will turned to a blank page in his notebook, and lifted it in the air momentarily as if to say to her, *I'm sure there's more.*

"Betty, you started out by saying that the workers need more money, but how much do they need?" asked Will.

"We can use anything we get," she said.

"If you say *that* to them, you'll get *nothing*. Now, what I want you to do is *tell* them what you are going to *demand,* and say it in a way that they know you mean business, and they will realize if they don't do what you ask, it's going to hurt them."

"Hurt *them*?"

"Yes, that's what you and your fellow workers need to understand. That mill is nothing without you. The owners make no money without you. They can't survive without you. You hold the control over their future if you stand together, okay?"

"I guess so."

"I'm going to suggest some demands in addition to all the things you just said: a twenty-five percent raise for all workers, two weeks paid vacation every year, four sick leave days per year; Christmas bonuses based on corporation profits—so the more profit the factory makes, the more bonus you receive. I also suggest that you demand new bathrooms with tiled floor and new fixtures. If the mill continues to have separate bathrooms for white and Negro workers, then the Negro bathrooms are to be made of the same material and same fixtures, and equal in size and accessibility as the white's. Also, demand that trees be planted that will provide shade on employee parking, and finally, exhaust fans mounted at the top of the walls of all large workrooms and equipment rooms."

"I don't know. Are we asking too much?" asked Betty.

"No, you are not *asking* for anything, These are *demand*s, your demands. It's what they owe you. You hold the reins," said Will.

# CHAPTER NINETEEN

## TRISH
## DECEMBER 1948

I didn't like being with Francis after work. Most of the time during the day, I was on my feet and I was just plain tired, but the thought of having to talk with Francis by myself after everybody had gone home was nerve-racking. It wasn't just me. None of the girls wanted to be with him alone for very long.

It was early in December and Francis sounded especially serious about something he wanted to talk about, and he said we had to be alone. After I had locked up, I waited a half hour for Francis to finish talking with Rebeca. Rebeca had never spoken to me — even then when I said goodbye, she only nodded and walked away. In the back room, Francis was sitting at his desk, which was exactly like Will's but on the opposite side of the room. Will's desk was always filled with stacks of paper, organized by date and by importance. Francis' desk was filled with papers scattered in no particular order as if he picked at random which project to work on next. In the middle of his desk was an uncluttered area exactly eighteen inches square that he used for writing. The only other clear area was a place reserved for the coffeepot and cup.

"Why don't you pull Will's chair over here," he said. I was afraid that meant we would be there late.

"What did you want to talk about?" I asked.

"Lots of stuff," he said exposing plenty of teeth, but not smiling. "Gonna change your job."

"Okay…is that good?

"Well, you're gonna work harder, keep part of your old responsibilities, and pick up more. You know Cynthia had to leave, and you've already picked up some of her work, but now we need you to do all the printing, writing, calling on the phone, and see that all correspondence is logged out, and recorded in, and things like that."

"I've never done all those things before… I mean for someone besides myself."

"Don't worry. We'll teach you."

"If I'm going to be working harder, and longer, I assume…"

"Money? You get more, okay?"

"Sure!"

"I write a lot of letters to Party members around the state and in South Carolina, and to other regions. I write regularly to Headquarters in New York, and I receive volumes of letters and information in response every week. Someone's got to keep them in order, and someone's got to help me with my grammar and spelling. Can you do that?"

"Yes."

"I also write lots of correspondence to people outside the Party."

"Who?"

"Many, many offshoots are surfacing everywhere and, like I said, I need your assistance to take my handwritten scribbling and make it a beautifully typed document. I need you to edit everything without changing my meaning, understand?"

"I think so, but who are these people if they are not connected to the Party? And what are *offshoots*?"

Francis closed the notebook in front of him and leaned toward me. He lowered his voice, even though there was no one else in the room to hear us, and said, "Trish, think about it for a while, but understand this one thing: even if, for some reason, we shut off our communication with Russia entirely, even if we cut off the CPUSA and NCCP totally, almost everybody in this country will eventually seek out the kind of reform and satisfaction that can only be found in socialism and eventually communism. Few people realize it, but there's a *need* for it, a deep, secret hunger for it, and lots of people are beginning to find it... Those are the off-shoots."

"So, are you saying socialism and communism are going to grow, no matter what happens to Russia, or the Party, or even to this country?"

"Exactly!"

"Are you saying this is the end of the Party? If so, why stick with it. Why have you spent so much time working for the Party? And why do you keep telling us that it's a good time to be a communist? Why don't we just take off, and each of us obey whatever we think is filling that *hunger* in our head?"

"I'm still telling you it *is* a great time to be a communist."

As far as I can remember, that was the first and only time I ever saw Francis smile. It was a completely self-satisfied look with his head cocked back and his eyes half closed. After a moment of soaking it in, he said, "It's in *everybody's head*, Trish. But to answer your question, as of today, CPUSA and the state organizations like NCCP are the most advanced engines of the communist culture available to us, but more things are rising around us now. Understand?" I shrugged my shoulders. He said, "Trish, you know I've been talking about these changes for a long time, but for now, just trust me. What I need for you to do is be my traffic cop for a while, and manage the volume of documents and correspondence that's going to be flooding through this office. There'll be more work, but I *will* pay more too. I've always told Will I thought I could trust you...Can you do the job?"

"Sure, I can do it." I heard my voice saying the words, but I didn't remember deciding that I actually wanted to do it, and I didn't believe that he always trusted me.

"What about the projects I'm working on now? Will I keep doing that work too in addition to the new work?"

"I'm going to give you *plenty* to do. I'll have to get another girl to take on most of your old projects."

"Did you ever make a decision about Jane Channing's request?" I asked.

"We can't get involved in that kind of project."

"Why? I thought it was a great idea. There are so many mill women who need child care, so they can work full time. Don't you think it would help give the Party a good name, especially with women?"

"Actually, it only affects about ten percent of the workers, so it's not a good place for us to spend our time and money. Channing's looking for help in raising funds for a bus to bring in children from other mills. We just don't get into those kinds of projects. But your work on the Durham Mill, and the Hillsboro Mill, and others will be continued by someone else."

"But I think…"

"I think we've talked about it enough. I've got a stack of papers for you to work on."

"Starting when?"

"Tomorrow. I'll be bringing you stacks of letters. I'll give you the names and addresses. And Trish…," he fixed his eyes on me long enough to let me know I had better remember what he was about to say, "The list of names is top secret. Never show it to anyone, not even Will, and don't ever question me about who these people are, okay?"

"Alright," I reluctantly muttered.

"Sometimes I'll call and read over the phone things for you to type. You'll jot them down, then type them up, and just like all the others, sign them for me and send them out."

"How can I sign for you? Is that legal?"

"I have a code name for you to use. You can just scribble my code name on everything that you send out, and nobody will know the difference."

"I don't know about that."

"It's no big deal. It's legal."

"What's the code name?"

"I'm not going to tell you until you agree to use it."

I couldn't see the harm if it was legal. "Okay, since it's not your name."

"The code name is, *Lisa B*."

"That's somebody's name!"

"Just a made-up name that I use sometimes."

I nodded, that seemed logical enough.

"Two more things, Trish. Be careful who you talk to about Party business and watch out for people who try to get close to you. Always be aware of strangers watching you."

"Okay, I will." I wondered if that had something to do with FBI agents snooping around the store.

"Also, *all* mail that comes in addressed to me *personally*, is to be placed in a safe file, unopened, and will be given to Rebecca each Wednesday and Friday."

"I know who she is, I saw her leave, but never met her."

"She's not the friendly type," he said.

"Should I log the items in?"

"No, you will not be able to tell who they are from by looking at the envelopes. Only Rebecca will take care of mail addressed to me. You will be responsible for everything that comes in for Lisa B. Got it?"

"Yes."

"Okay then, one final thing you will do for me. I frequently need to have packages delivered to a contact in Raleigh. You and the contact will work out the details about when and where you two will meet. Only you two will know, and you must be sure you are not followed. Okay?

"Yes, but Raleigh is only forty-five minutes away. Why do you need *me* to do it? Why not Rebecca?"

"Because I want *you* to do it."

"Can I ask why so secret?"

"No...But I can tell you it's about the work we're doing for the Jefferson School in New York. I'm sure you've heard about it over the last few years."

"Yes, but just from you and Will."

"We're trusting you. You *will not* fail me on this."

He looked at me as if waiting for some kind of assurance that I got the message — or the threat.

"I understand," I said.

•••

In addition to my administrative duties, keeping up with correspondence, and printing, I kept a calendar on my desk. Will and Francis fought over blocks of my schedule. Francis started spending more time on the road and delegating more work to me, including making deposits and sending out checks to pay bills.

Francis never got over Henry Wallace losing his bid for President, but he saw an opportunity to plan a resurgence of the socialist agenda on the national scene in the 1952 elections. He anticipated that the coming years would be very busy for us, and he predicted Eisenhower would run, and be very strong competition. Because of Eisenhower's anticommunist stand, the CPUSA declared him a prime target to write about in our propaganda.

I worked harder and longer each day. Writing Francis's code name became as easy as writing my own name.

# CHAPTER TWENTY

## TRISH
## JANUARY 1949

We couldn't believe the University had agreed to let John Gates lecture at Graham Memorial Hall. Francis told me to create color posters, and plaster them around the campus, using the title, *A CELEBRATION OF FREE SPEECH*. I was to include a simple paragraph saying, *John Gates, A Prominent member of the Communist Party Headquarters in New York, will speak at Graham Hall on Friday, January 12, at 7:00. Come to hear this inspiring talk about the shifting of American politics.*

We canceled all of the usual Friday field trips to be there early for the speech. We all ate dinner together and drove caravan-style back downtown. Since it was January, and there were no sports events going on that night, everyone found parking places on Franklin Street close to the bookstore. Our enthusiasm was so high that we didn't notice how fast the temperature was dropping as evening approached. We marched to the hall like victorious soldiers forty-five minutes before the lecture was to begin. Some students, and others, were already there when we arrived. But the front doors were locked and the building was dark. Within ten minutes there were at least one-hundred people waiting outside, and by a quarter of seven, there must have been a thousand. That's when Fran and Will walked up with John Gates, who they had picked up at the airport.

Since Gates, along with eleven other communists, had already been arraigned in New York, he had to catch a flight to Raleigh from the Trenton Airport in New Jersey instead of flying out of New York. He had to use an assumed name to avoid any attention.

Someone in the crowd recognized Francis and handed him a note. His face turned red as he looked over the paper and gave it to John Gates. They exchanged a few whispers, and Francis climbed onto the base of the massive column on the extreme right of the porch, the column where I used to feed Bearcat in the mornings. Francis's high-pitched voice pierced the cold air like a whip.

He said, "We've been given a note that says the administration has changed their minds about allowing John Gates to lecture tonight," An instant roar rose from the crowd with some boos, some angered garble, and some laughter. "This, as you   know…," he paused to add drama for a crowd already glued to whatever he was going to say, "is a speech they had already agreed to. Apparently, while our speaker was on his way here, they reneged on their courage, and open-mindedness." Another roar echoed through the courtyard. "We're here to celebrate one of our great American rights, free speech, and we see no reason why this kind of stubborn resistance to our rights should keep this speech from being given." Another round of jeers and cheers. "So, let's march, all of us together, two blocks from here, off campus, to the old schoolhouse building on Franklin Street. You will *have* your speech!" All cheered and stepped aside so Francis, Will, and John could lead the way. My group was immediately lost in the crowd, but we managed to keep within twenty feet or so of Francis, as he made his way through the campus. A group of boys on my left sang out a made-up chant, *"Free speech, free speech..."* and almost immediately a group on the right chanted back in jest, *"Get a rope, get a rope..."* Most of the crowd, however, marched silently with the excitement of a rare event held in the chilly January night air.

All chanting stopped when we crossed Columbus Street. Francis climbed a stone wall in front of the old school building. He helped Gates and Will climb to the top of the wall where everyone could see him. The flock gathered across the base of the wall and filled Franklin Street—completely blocking all traffic. The local police immediately appeared, and started redirecting cars from Franklin Street, to Rosemary Street and all traffic on Columbus Street was turned back to Cameron Avenue. There must have been a full two-thousand people filling the streets.

The crowd roared when Francis stepped forward to introduce John Gates. The rumbling and chanting stopped when Gates held up his hand. His voice was powerful and clear enough for all to hear every word. The moist, cold air around us, and the glare of street lights turned every word he spoke into a bright smoky mist puffing from his mouth, like the exhaust from a steam engine.

"I want to thank the University for throwing us off the campus and giving us a perfect case-in-point, proving that their intractable mindset is to control your free thinking by prohibiting any presentation or discussion about alternative forms of society and government. Their action tonight shows the school's continuing need to punish those who challenge authority and repress those who despise outgrown laws."

A cheer rose from a small group far behind me.

Gates continued, "What kind of university would want their students to believe that there is only one way to see things?"

Another cheer rang out from the same group.

"What university would permit no vision of the future's infinite possibilities?"

A grumble of protesting voices rose around us drowning out the small group behind me.

"What university would consciously stifle progressive thinking in student minds?" he said turning toward his supporters. "Is that what you want from the University of North Carolina? Is that the kind of atmosphere in which you expected to invest four years of your life—your primary learning years?" He raised an open hand to the crowd.

"You all know who your US senators and congressmen are, right? Then send a letter of protest to all of them. Send them lots of letters and inform them that the staff and faculty of this university are choking away your right to a balanced education and discouraging any conversation that includes progressive thinking. Write to them also to repeal the Smith Act which is, in *itself*, a violation of the First Amendment. As you may know, I and ten of my colleagues have been arraigned for violating the Smith Act—an act that is silencing and incarcerating our best thinkers. Even as I stand here now, I could be arrested at any moment. In contrast with what the Act implies, I'm *not* seeking the *violent* overthrow of the US Government.

The goal is a fundamental replacement of the way the country works and centralizing authority into a simple socialist government."

The pack behind me cheered again, but the remainder of the crowd blasted back with boos, hoots, and an angry roar. The pack yelled louder and the crowd responded with earsplitting screams.

Gates raised his hand again until everyone was silent, then said, "I am told the University of North Carolina has a history of students who explore progressive thinking, some embrace it and some don't. I ask only to be heard tonight. You may not like what I say but give us a few minutes to stretch your minds. Give us a chance to tell you things you have not heard or do not yet understand, then go home and think about it and forget about me."

For the next ten or fifteen minutes, Gates described what the future of the country could be like as a fully operating communist society: how poverty, greed, fighting between parties and factions could be eliminated, and how fear and worry of the future would become extinct. Because I was so short, I couldn't see what the mob around me was doing, but I heard an increasing grumble and shuffling feet.

As soon as Gates finished speaking, Francis stepped forward and called out for questions. The students wasted no time asking about significant points in his speech. They asked for an expansion of the subtle innuendos he implied and wanted more of his vision of the country's future under communism. While he was answering, someone threw a large white object that arced high over the street and smashed against the head of a man standing beside me. As he fell, he bumped his head on the wall, and then bounced to the sidewalk. He was unconscious a few moments. I knelt beside him to be sure he was okay. Two officers helped Gates, Will, and Francis down from the wall, then ushered them through the crowd. I held the injured man's head, waiting for two other officers to take him away. As the police escorted John, Will, and Francis through the pack, Gates' supporters continually fell in line and marched behind them as they shouted out words I didn't understand or just too afraid to hear. The remainder of the mob yelled back an angry spontaneous response. The crowd had gone from silent listening to an explosion of voices all around me. Gates' supporters pushed the crowd in the direction he was being escorted, while the opponents shoved away from him. This started the whole mob churning in a counter-clockwise motion like one big machine. I fought my way back to the side of the concrete wall and, along with others trying to avoid the stampede, I managed to climb on top. From there I looked over the horde that filled both streets.

Everybody was shouting and no one was listening. Fists were rising into the air in all directions. I was the only worker for the Party on the wall. I couldn't see any of my friends that came with me that night. I recognized no one; every face looked the same, and I felt like they were all angry at *me*.

Because of the limited space on top of the wall, I was getting pushed closer and closer to the edge as more people climbed up to escape the crush. Because I was so much shorter than they were, they probably didn't even notice me standing there, digging in my heels, and pushing back into the men behind me. But they just pushed harder causing me to inch closer over the edge.

After a few minutes, I noticed a tall man on the far side of Franklin Street plowing through the crowd straight toward me. I couldn't see his face, but from his size, determination and strength, I knew it was Lem. He called my name with his deep thundering voice. I waved. When he finally elbowed his way close to the wall, he yelled, "Give me your hands." Not knowing what he had in mind, I held both arms in front of me. He grabbed my right elbow and yelled, "Jump." I hesitated. "Jump now!" he roared again. Obediently I leaned forward and then leaped. Still holding my right arm, he grabbed my left thigh, just above the knee. In the crush of the crowd, there was not enough room to lower me, so he held me face down, high above his head, and started a power march back through the mob. As he walked against the crowd, they parted to get out of his way, leaving him a clear path. In Lem's giant hands, I floated at least eight feet above the ground. I watched the faces of students passing beneath me. They all stared forward in the direction in which they were being pushed as if someone up front actually knew where they were going.

With both arms stretched out, I must have looked like I was flying. A group of students on the other side of Franklin Street apparently recognized me as the girl from the bookstore, because they cheered and sang out my name in rhythm as if my dramatic exit from the stage was a great closing act for the bizarre nighttime event.

Away from the crowd on the sidewalk on the far side of Columbus Street, I saw Tim Horn standing perfectly still watching Lem carry me away. As soon as Lem lowered me to the ground, we ran up the street to our car.

He didn't say a single word on the way home, but I

heard from his body language all I needed to know. He almost never got angry, but when he did, he steamed inside, and his breathing became strong and rhythmic. After we pulled in behind his truck in our driveway, he went immediately to his room, and I didn't see him again for the rest of the night.

It wasn't possible for me to sleep. In bed, I rehearsed apologies with convincing explanations about my ignorance and my immaturity. I practiced promises that I thought he could accept. At daybreak, I waited in my room long enough for Lem to finish his chores. Through the window, I watched the sun rising behind slow-moving clouds. In the kitchen, there was no sign that Lem had made breakfast. Down at the pen, the ducks had all been fed and Lem's truck was gone. I went back to my bed, cried for a while, then drove to work.

Lem didn't talk to me for a week. I know he wanted to, but words never came to him easily, and I'm sure he was so angry he would say all the wrong things until he cooled down.

By 9:00 the following morning, Will had finished writing an article for the communist paper, *The Daily Worker,* on John Gates' speech emphasizing the students' enthusiastic support and acceptance of certain ideas in the speech. He gave me the handwritten copy, which I edited, and typed up a final draft before taking it to be Teletyped to the New York Headquarters for inclusion in the next printing of the newspaper. The following day, however, the campus paper, *The Daily Tar Heel,* published a full account of the event, describing how the large crowd cried out with both boos and cheers, and how they marched off campus to hear a speech from the noted communist John

Gates. The article went on to say that, as a whole, the event felt more like a football pep rally than a political speech.

Two days later *The Greensboro Daily* came out with a similar article, except it was written from the viewpoint of the *Greensboro Daily's* reporter who was knocked out by the white object thrown by someone in the crowd. The reporter pointed out that the missile was intended to hit John Gates, but even though it missed Gates, it still symbolized the student's strong opposition to his message. He also said that the white object that hit him in the head was a roll of wet toilet paper.

Before Francis arrived at the store the next morning, Carole and I laid the two newspapers on Francis's desk opened to the articles about the speech.

Francis arrived through the back entrance that morning. He didn't bother to tell us he was there, but we knew it when we heard the newspapers smashing against the back of the workroom door. He calmed down by midmorning, and he and Will spent the day writing rebuttals, which they gave to me at the end of the day to be edited and typed immediately. The following morning, the local *Chapel Hill Weekly*, which was delivered to our doorstep each Thursday, had three articles along with pictures filling the front page. Each article shouted exaggerated claims of the dangerous activities of the Communist Party in Chapel Hill with its headquarters in the Community Book Store on Franklin Street. The biggest picture on the front page was a shot of me, coming out of the bookstore carrying a pack of pamphlets. The article included my name, Francis's name, Will's name, and no one else.

# CHAPTER TWENTY-ONE

## TRISH
## FEBRUARY 1949

I knew dozens of UNC students by name, and they knew me and recognized me from the store and from my morning walks around the campus.

Because of the recent articles and the event in front of the old high school on Franklin Street, the university made a decision that all communists and all workers for the Party would be banned. They also declared that no one who had ever worked for the Party would be allowed on the university staff or faculty. The local businesses posted lists of names and pictures of people they would not allow in their establishment. My face and name were on every window and door of every restaurant and shop. Because I had worked in the store so long and had been so visible, there were more pictures of me than Will, Francis, or anyone else in the store.

I felt mentally and physically numb as I walked down Franklin Street. People that never knew me, recognized me from the pictures scattered around the town and stared at me like they were afraid I would brainwash them on the spot. People that knew me for years, looked away as if they never met me.

An endless, empty cavern opened inside me. I thought at first, I could get over it by staying home on the farm for a few days, but when Lem saw the newspapers, he was so furious he stopped talking to me entirely. He treated me like I was dead. On the coffee table in the living room, he left the front pages of the Chapel Hill, Durham, and Raleigh newspapers showing my name and picture. I wished he had yelled at me or stomped around and threw objects against the wall—anything to help him blow off his disappointment in me, but he just boiled inside his big head and stomach. The following week, *The Raleigh Times* continued its attack with a picture of me in the store. The headline read, *Communists still Threaten Chapel Hill*. That was enough to finally throw Lem over the edge. His voice roared so loud, it hurt my ears.

*"Trish, how did this happen to you? Why didn't you tell me what you were doin'? You gotta stop. I don't know who you are now!"* he continued to fire off questions without giving me a chance to answer.

I fell on the couch and buried my head under pillows, but his relentless blast vibrated the room. Bearcat pushed his way through the screen door and ran into the yard.

"Lem! I *told* you I'm not a communist. I don't get involved in a lot of things they do. I just help with . . ."

"It doesn't matter what you do! It's wrong, *wrong*," he said as he slammed his fist on the table.

"You still don't know *anything* about it, do you?"

He shook his head as he said, "All I know about communism is what I've heard from my friends and from the radio. There has been lots of talk 'bout it over the last five years or so, and I don't hear anything that's good."

"But they're trying to . . ."

140

"I know what they're *tryin'* to do! But you've been duped, *fooled*, and… God only knows what else. You're an easy target for these people. Trish, you need to get out of there."

"No, I'm not a target! I know what I'm doing, and I know what I want to accomplish, and it can't be done here on this duck farm. Do you understand?"

"I'll tell you what I understand. When you're on the farm, you at least *try* to think for yourself, but I don't know who's thinkin' for you when you leave."

"When I'm at Chapel Hill, I think about making other people's lives better."

"So do I. I help people. I raise somethin' for them to eat."

"How many of those people have you actually met?" I asked. He didn't answer. "They mean *nothing* to you."

Lem stepped in front of me, glared down at me, and said with a demanding but constrained voice, "What I do doesn't hurt anybody. What you do, sooner or later, hurts everyone."

I couldn't control myself. I jumped to my feet and ran into his precious trophy room, picked up a stuffed fox, and threw it through the door onto the living-room floor. It bounced and slid against Lem's feet. One of the glass eyes popped out and rolled under the table. I did the same thing to his favorite raccoon. "Do you know what these things are, Lem?" He ran into the room without replying. I spread out my arms and extended my fingers as if I were pointing to all of the animals around me. I screamed at him and said, "These are symbols of your career. You grow beautiful little ducks just to *kill* them along with all these poor stuffed creatures. All I want to do is make *somebody's* life better. I'll never be a duck farmer. What you are trying to do right now, is take away from me the only thing I have ever accomplished in my life outside of this farm. Don't you see, take it away, and I am *nothing!*"

He didn't say a word as he picked the two animals off the floor and inspected them for damage, then carefully put them back in their places. He stormed out of the house, leaving me alone surrounded by his trophies staring at me. I watched him through the living-room window as he walked with Bearcat by his side, around the north end of the pond, and up the hill to the graveyard. I was glad he was gone because it would calm him down and would also give me the chance I desperately needed to get hold of myself. I had never spoken to him like that before. I didn't know where it came from, but it didn't matter. I couldn't stand thinking about how much I had hurt him. Within minutes, Lem returned. The first thing he said was, "*How* could you do this to Mom and Dad?"

"I didn't do it to . . ."

"Yes, you *did*. How do you think everybody that knew them feel right now? How about your aunt and uncle? How about all our friends, all their neighbors, and all the people at church. By now, everyone knows about it. What could I ever say to them? You robbed the family of things we'll never get back...*Never!*"

"Lem, *please* listen to me!" He was beyond listening. I tried for another half hour and it all grew worse, and his yelling grew louder. I had never, never seen him like that.

At the end, he was spitting out his thoughts so fast, the only thing I understood was , "You gotta *go!*" After that, dense silence. I fell back on the couch again and covered my head. When I sat up, Lem was gone. I looked through the window and saw him and Bearcat going into the duck pens.

There was not a moment in my life that I didn't love my big brother, my best friend… who threw me out of my house that day. I filled the car with as much of my belongings as I could. Our long curving driveway ends at Chicken Bridge Road. I stopped about a hundred yards from the road, fell over in the front seat to clear my head. I don't know how many hours went by, but the starless night completely swallowed me and my car. I stepped outside and tried to breathe. There was nothing for me to see or hear anywhere—just me, and the car, night sounds, and black air surrounding me.

The only place I could go was back to Chapel Hill. I finished the night in the parking area in front of Will's apartment. The sun had just risen when Will tapped on my window. I explained all that had happened at the farm and that I had no place to go.

Many times, over the last few years, Will offered the spare room in his apartment if I ever needed it, and finally, I needed it. I tried to apologize, but he wouldn't let me.

"You may not remember," he said, "I warned you that the t-time would come when you would lose all your friends even those closest to you. I'm so sorry it had to be Lem. I know what he has meant to you your whole life, and there's nothing I could say that will ease that p-pain right now, except that I understand it, and I will do all I can to help you get through it."

He cleaned out a small room that he had used as an office. At first, I had to sleep on a mattress on the floor until he bought a new bed for me. He purchased everything I needed and would not let me pay him back. I still made money at the store, but he wouldn't take any of it and told me to save it for the future.

From then on, I spent all my time working for the cause.

# CHAPTER TWENTY-TWO

## TRISH
### JULY 1950

Francis and Will wrote articles every other day for newspapers around the state, for *The Daily Worker*, and for *The Daily Tarheel*. As always, Francis saw a time of great opportunity for the Party, a new acceptance of socialist ideals. The Korean War suddenly erupted, and Francis launched a campaign blitz to rouse the minds of Carolinians to understand what he felt was the real cause of the war. He started a new paper calling it *Fighter for Peace*. He made it small enough to be mailed across the four states surrounding us. He also gave it away wherever he could. He railed against America's motive for entering the war and claimed that the whole war was designed to exploit and extend the already established US imperialism and to further oppress the Negro people by drafting them into the army disproportionately compared to whites. He insisted the whole war was manufactured to support an illegitimate nation in South Korea.

During that same period of time, Russia successfully completed testing their first nuclear bomb, and the world awoke to realize there were two atomic powers competing with each other. As a result, an international resolution, known as the Stockholm Peace Petition, was drafted in Sweden by the World Peace Council outlawing the use of atomic weapons and stating that *any government that employs such weapons will be dealt with as a war criminal.* Francis designed and wrote the text for pamphlets condemning the United States for rejecting the Stockholm Petition, and he circulated the pamphlets along with his own petition encouraging others to register their protest. He collected over a thousand signatures throughout both Carolinas and surrounding states. This caused the *Durham Sun* to write an article blasting the NCCP for turning people against our country's efforts. The paper said, *The Communist Party and its members are our enemies, and they need to be captured and brought to justice. We are at war now, and our nation's well-being is at risk. We call on North Carolinians to join our request to have these people locked up for the duration of the Korean War.*

Francis packed up several boxes of his pamphlets as well as the petition. He instructed Gill Holstrum and his crew to take them to Raleigh to the general assembly building and do whatever it took to make the elected officials hear our message.

We didn't find out until the next day that Holstrum's gang had been arrested. The initial charge was disorderly conduct, but the FBI quickly stepped in and charged them with sedition. The morning after their arrest, an article came out in the *Raleigh Times* about their violent behavior, listing each one by their full names. The newspaper also said they had been told by a reliable source that the four men were members of the Communist Party.

I said to Will, "Holstrum is the most aggressive, explosive guy in our group. Why did Francis select *him* and his gang to go to the State House? Right now, is the worst time I can imagine to do something like that. I thought Francis had better sense."

"This *is* the worst time, and Holstrum *is* the worst person to do it, and Francis *knew* what would happen."

"You mean…"

"Yes, he set them up."

"Did you know about that before they left for Raleigh?"

"Yes, and I warned them, but Holstrum was too stupid, and Francis was too clever."

"He wanted them arrested?"

"That's my guess. He's been looking for an opportunity to get rid of Holstrum and his followers for a long time."

"Why would Francis do something that would make the Party look bad?"

"I'm only guessing, but I believe he thought it would focus public attention on the issues we are proposing, and at the same time, sacrifice Holstrum."

I tried to stay away from Francis as much as I could, although I didn't mind the additional work. It took my mind off Lem and off the way I left the farm.

Throughout the summer, controversy concerning communist control of the Local 22 Union at Reynolds Tobacco plant continued to heat up until it reached a point where criticism from newspapers around the state took on a hysterical tone. Over the radio, the mayor of Winston Salem referred to the local Communist Party as *Stalin's songbirds* and demanded they be *driven from our doorsteps.* In August the National Labor Relations Board voted to expel the Local 22 union completely cutting off the communist influence at the plant and ending the NCCP's largest and longest project.

# CHAPTER TWENTY-THREE

## TRISH
## FEBRUARY 1952

On a cloudy Saturday, at Francis's request, I rode with him to the North Carolina College at Durham. He said he needed help with a rally there, and I obediently obliged. He never said what the rally was for, and I didn't bother to ask—but that wasn't unusual. Francis always seemed to have a few secrets tucked away in his pockets. I had been to the college before with Will for other events, and since it was a Negro college, he always asked the college for permission to pass out leaflets on campus. Francis, however, believed he didn't need to ask anybody's permission for anything, and his personal view of justice superseded all man-made restrictions or formalities.

We parked and followed a walkway through the center of the campus. A clamor of yelling voices echoed off the buildings. A slight breeze blew sheets of paper across the grass toward us. As one of the papers blew closer, I saw the words *Korean War* on it, so I picked it up and read the message.

"What's this?" I exclaimed.

Francis grunted, "Our handouts. I had them printed here, and we're giving them out right now,"

He picked one up, looked at it for a moment, and tossed it back on the ground. I stood still as he walked on.

"Come on!" he commanded and waved his arm.

I stood still and read the paper a little further. "Francis!" I called out, but he didn't stop walking. "Francis, this is a blood drive for the soldiers. Is that what we're protesting?" I said without moving. The voices bouncing around the buildings became louder and angrier.

He marched back to me pumping his arms like he was preparing for a fight. He said, "This is a protest against the *War!*"

"I could see that from the flyer, but this blood drive is for our soldiers. You don't have any problems with them, do you?"

"I don't have time to argue. Come with me." He deepened his voice and tightened his fists.

I noticed a banner taped on the building wall behind him that said, "*American Red Cross, Blood Drive for our Troops in Korea.*"

"Francis, tell me why we're doing this!"

He rolled his head back and glared at me through the bottom of his eyelids, then slowly blew through his lips and said, "You don't have any idea what's going on, do you?"

"Well, obviously, these people here are giving blood for our soldiers, and we're staging some kind of protest to stop it."

"And did you see a blood drive at UNC?"

"No."

"Why do you think they are doing the blood drive at the Negro college?"

"I assume they are doing it wherever they can…What's

wrong with that?"

"Why don't you see what our government is doing? They are, yet again, exploiting, what we call, the *Negro Nation* to fight in a war created to serve only one possible purpose — to generate more wealth for the capitalist in this country, and at what price? The price of the *blood* of *these* people."

"That's crazy! If blood is needed for the troops, and these students want to give it why not let them."

"The government knows these people will give blood because so many of their fellow students, disproportionately compared to the white colleges, have been pulled away from their studies and made to fight."

"Where did you get that piece of information?"

"My channels."

"Through the Party?"

"Of course."

I felt my cheeks burning, and I'm sure I must have turned red as a radish. He started to say something, but I cut him off by saying, "I read somewhere that we're battling the North Koreans, but what we are actually fighting is Russian control over the North Korean Government, right?"

"Yes, so what?"

"*Fighting Russia* is your problem with all this, *isn't* it?"

"It's not just about that, and you know it."

"What I *don't* know is *why* I'm here!"

By that time, three of our workers, two men, and one woman, joined us and they were eager to tell Francis about how many leaflets had been handed out and describe some of the conversations they had with the students. I had seen the two men before but didn't know their names. The woman was Rebecca. They all three talked simultaneously like children just arriving home from summer camp. Telling their new accomplishments to Francis Schoberg was a big deal to them, and Francis seemed to be pleased that some of the students at the College were listening to his people and reading the propaganda. Francis assumed the enthusiasm of the three young workers would cure my reluctance to participate in the protest.

The air was cold, but I felt hot under my jacket. I needed to get away from Francis and the other guys. "Can I have some of those leaflets?" I asked. Each of the three gave me a handful of the flyers. "I see some women over in the corner of the courtyard. I think I'll try to approach them."

Just as I looked back at Francis, several flashes from a newspaper reporter's camera lit our faces. "You guys better get back to work," Francis said to the three. He looked pleased, probably thinking I had been persuaded. He turned and walked back toward the crowd and disappeared between two brick buildings. The reporter followed him. I handed the flyers back to the three men, and they walked away leaving me alone.

Shouts came from behind me, and a large group of students from the Durham college stomped their way up the sidewalk. I stepped off the pavement to let them pass.

"What are you doing?" one of then asked.

"I'm...I'm a reporter," I said softly. If I said it any louder, it would have sounded like the lie that it was.

"So why are you standing here?" they asked as they slowed down to a near stop.

"I'm afraid," I said and by then, I really was afraid, and I'm sure they could hear it in my voice.

After whispering to the others, one of the young men

said to me, "Walk behind us. You'll be okay."

I was more afraid to stand there alone than I was to walk behind them. So I obediently marched with them, down the walk, around the buildings, and through an arched passageway leading to a large open space. On one side, stood a building that housed the campus bookstore and student center. I assumed most of the other buildings were dormitories or academic buildings. On a concrete plaza outside the bookstore, official looking men wearing suits sat behind two long tables. Three women in nurse's uniforms, scurried back and forth escorting students into and out of booths. To the right side of the tables, was a long line of students waiting to be taken into one of the booths to give blood. I recognized three of our workers handing out leaflets. One carried a sign. The chanting and protesting continued from a group of about twenty of our men in the center of the quadrangle. I recognized half of them. They marched in a wide circle that blocked the main walkway preventing the students from crossing the plaza.

The pack of young men I was following sped up their deliberate pace as they headed for the middle of the protest line. Soon, other students from the college joined us, creating a giant human wedge with me in the dead center. I was so short, I couldn't see what was going on around us, and I'm sure no one could see me. We marched straight toward the circle of protesters, splitting the circle in half, and causing them to stop in their tracks. The protesters continued chanting, but no longer sounding like an angry mob—more like a boy's catechism recital.

That's when I saw that some protesters were already quietly slipping away. When the rest of the workers saw their size dwindling on both ends, they started walking, then trotting, then fleeing toward the exits in all corners of the quadrangle. The wedge of students surrounding me cheered as the protesters ran away.

No one spoke to me as I walked back by the men giving blood. I walked past the booths, around the corners of the brick buildings, and down the long sidewalk toward the parking lot where Francis had parked his car. I recognized some of the workers' cars as they flew out of the lot. Francis and his car were already gone.

I walked back into the quadrangle, hoping one of my friends would give me a ride. I looked all over for someone I knew, but they were all gone. The sound of conflict around the campus turned into sounds of celebration. Again, I was alone.

"Need a ride?" I heard a male voice say, but I didn't answer or move. "Need a ride, Trish?" he said again. I tuned. It was Timothy Horn.

"Yes, please, I think I was left behind."

"By Francis?"

"Yep."

He shook his head and said, "I'm ready. Let's go."

I was out of breath when I jumped into the front seat of Tim's car. My hand was shaking as I unzipped my jacket halfway down. I don't remember driving out of Durham at all, and we were on the highway before I finally caught my breath and said, "What was that?"

"What was what?"

"What was that circus we just left? What was it all about? What were we doing there?" I shouted. Tim looked over at me and said nothing. I couldn't tell if he felt the same way or was offended by my comment. I watched the road for a few more minutes and contemplated jumping out of the car.

Finally, he said, "Circus is a good word for it. Did you read the flyers?"

"Yes."

"Then you know the answer why we were there."

"That event helped nobody. Nobody!" I said as I pulled my collar over my face trying to hide my tears and silence my sobbing breath.

"I agree," he said, "but what did you expect?"

"I don't know. It was pure insanity.

"*Insanity*. Another good word."

I fought back another round of emotions and rested my forehead against the cool glass window and watched plowed fields and farmhouses go by. Tim made a right turn and stopped the car. We were in front of a block building painted white with a big sign that said, *Burgers, Fries, and Shakes*.

"What kind of shake do you like? He asked.

"Do you think they have strawberry?"

"I'll see," he said, as he hopped out. In no time, he returned with two large cups in his hand. "Strawberry," he said handing one of the cups to me.

I thanked him, and we sat there for another five minutes. The only sound was slurping.

"I feel better," I said.

"Yes, any kind of milkshake is really good medicine for whatever's bothering you," he said with a laugh.

"I'm going to need a lot more shakes, I think, to heal what's bothering me."

"Can you tell me?"

"Probably not."

"Is it the Party?"

"That's got a lot to do with it."

"What about the Party bothers you?"

"Well…it's actually… I don't think I know you well enough to tell you how I feel, so tell me what *you* think about all this."

"An *insane circus*."

"In your own words."

"Okay, the Party took a step backward today. Watch and see what happens. I would not be surprised to hear that all the local papers are blasting us and calling us *traitors*. I'm glad you wanted to get out of there."

"So did you leave because of me? I asked.

"No, but you helped me decide."

For the next hour, he asked me all about the things I had done for the Party, and what it was like to grow up on a duck farm, and what I hoped to do in the future—which was impossible for me to answer.

I replied, "You realize I know almost nothing about you, except that you came from Wake Forest, and you're studying history, or something like that at UNC. You've got previous experience with the Party, and you aren't married. So, other than that, who are you?"

"That's pretty much it. I'm really rather boring. I'm actually a graduate student in history, and I received my undergraduate degree at Wake Forest. I have no family to speak of, and I've been engaged but never married—too much of a bookworm I guess."

He had big hands and broad shoulders—not built like a book-worm. "How did you manage to stay out of the war?"

"Well,…" he hesitated. "to pay some of my tuition, I worked for a couple of years for a company who made the material used in parachutes and, kind of like your brother, I got an exemption just long enough to keep me out."

We were getting close to Chapel Hill and I let the conversation stop there. I searched my mind trying to remember any time over the all the years I was in Chapel Hill that I told anybody about Lem's exemption from the draft. I had never mentioned it to anybody, yet he threw it out like it was old news. Why did he ask so many questions about me, and give so little about himself? For the second time that day, I felt like jumping out of the car. He let me out in town near my parking space. The moment I got into my car, I locked the door and drove back to Will's apartment. I told him everything that happened in Durham. He was a good listener and tried to reassure me that it would all look different in the morning. The following day, I was at work doing everything Francis asked.

Jack Hemphill

# CHAPTER TWENTY-FOUR

## WILL
## MAY 1952

"*What's this*?" asked Trish looking at the stacks of boxes on the floor of the workroom.

"Paper," I answered.

"You've never bought this much before. What's up?"

"We're gonna get Vincent Hallinan elected!"

"*We* are?"

"Yes, the Progressive Party asked us to help get him elected P-President."

"Election is only six months away! Don't you think it's a little late for that?"

"Well, we're going to be the number one, and maybe the only, distributor of campaign material in the Carolinas."

"You know he doesn't have a chance?" she asked.

"Yes... no, well the Progressive P-Party asked for our help, and you get to print it. I'll distribute it, and we'll see what happens next."

"*You're* going to distribute it?"

"I've got people scattered around who are eager to work with us."

"So what exactly are we printing?"

"T-Ten thousand leaflets and one-hundred poster size

prints. How's our supply of ink?"

"I'll check it right now," she said as she turned to look into the supply cabinets.

I heard Trish give out a long sigh. "I know it sounds like a lot of work," I said. She just nodded. After finishing her brief inventory, she sat on the chair beside my desk.

"We're going to need more paper, and ink, and everything else. But Will, it feels like we're trying to glue wings on a turtle, you know what I mean? What's the point? It's not going to fly. You know Hallinan hasn't a chance. We both know Eisenhower is going to win, don't we?"

"Probably, but Adlai Stevenson will come in s-second, and I predict Hallinan will come in third. Did you know there are *six* parties this year with candidates running for president, and four of the six parties have strong socialist agendas and all four are backing socialist candidates?"

"*Six* parties? No, I didn't know that."

"In addition to the usual D-Democrats and Republicans, we have the *Progressive Party* with Vincent Hallinan, *Socialist Party* with Darlington Hoops, *Socialist Labor Party* with Eric Hass, and the *Socialist Worker's Party* with Farrell Dobbs, all running for president—strong socialists. So, you see, our message is getting out there, and it's popping up in different ways."

"But what chance does any of them have against Eisenhower?"

"Doesn't matter. Don't worry about it, Trish. It's getting the message out there that counts, at least for now. You see that don't you?"

"I suppose so. It's just all that work in six months seems like a lot to take on right now."

"It *is* a lot, but I have great confidence we can do it."

"Thanks, I wish I knew how," she said.

"You've done a lot for us, Trish. You're a very strong woman. I t-told you that a long time ago."

"I'll do my best, but I'll need some help. Can I have Jackie?"

"Okay, you got her."

Trish worked her tail off. The new girl, Jackie, was a big help, and I stayed late with Trish helping with the printing whenever I could.

Trish was the best thing that ever happened to me. She never asked for anything, but I made sure she had whatever she wanted. When she left the farm, she left almost all of her clothes behind, and so I bought her a whole new wardrobe for every season. She was the only person who was ever willing to live with me, and I think the only person that ever understood me, or at least tried to understand me. I hated the thought of ever losing her.

# CHAPTER TWENTY-FIVE

## TRISH
## JUNE 1952

Within a couple of months, I knew every registered communist in the Carolinas by name, plus some very active socialists and many members of the Progressive Party. I knew what they were all working on, and how they planned to accomplish it.

I knew all the major players in the entire southern region including North and South Carolina, Tennessee, Virginia, and the northern part of Mississippi; and soon after that, I was corresponding directly with the office of the head of CPUSA in New York.

I never knew where Francis lived, but it must have been somewhere not far from Chapel Hill because he came to our little office behind the store at odd hours and at unpredictable times. He always had a fist full of scribbled notes and letters for me to type. Will, on the other hand, typed and sent out most of his own letters, but he always gave me carbon copies for the file. I somehow managed to decipher Francis's scratchings and correct his English and grammar well enough for it to appear worthy of the NCCP Chairman. By the end of the year, however, in addition to his usual contacts, he had created a separate network of people. I noticed a very different tone in his language when he wrote to those individuals. It was hard for me to identify what it was, even though he received replies from them daily. I wasn't allowed to open letters addressed to him by name, so I saved them in a special file. I kept a log of all correspondence.

That same year, Francis bought a 35mm camera and taught me to use it with the instructions that I was to make a photo record of all our documents, events, meetings, rallies, and fights on picket lines. I never asked why he wanted it, but I enjoyed using the camera. All forms or contracts were photographed, printed, and filed. I also made photos of all letters from New York, so we would have extra copies. When documents required a witness, Will and Francis insisted that I sign them using my personal name.

As the Korean War continued to escalate, Francis became more agitated and vocal in his opposition to the war. His writing became more vigorous and even more profane. I, of course, smoothed over his language without telling him.

Francis subscribed to newspapers in Raleigh, Durham, Winston-Salem, Charlotte, and Wilmington in North Carolina; and Columbia and Charleston in South Carolina. It was part of my job to search for news articles and editorials that targeted the Party. Opposition seemed to be popping up everywhere. Even at the bookstore in Chapel Hill, the friendly discussions and debates gradually became angry, and finally were abandoned. Sales in the bookstore declined. People and institutions that had previously been silent raised their voices and wrote articles condemning our goals. The Party fought back with more propaganda, more newspaper articles, and some radio broadcasts. This only made the voices against us louder and more threatening.

The Durham Sun wrote another article saying, *We Americans here in North Carolina, have been tolerant and forbearing enough. We are in a national emergency.*

*The Communist Party of the United States is a division of the Communist Party in Russia. Its members are our enemies. It is time they were rounded up and rendered harmless. We call on the State and the Federal Government to take into custody the leaders of NCCP and all identified with it.*

I couldn't imagine what the writer for the *Durham Times* meant by saying that *America had been tolerant* and forbearing *enough.* Most of my life I had been isolated in one way or another. Growing up on the farm, having Lem as a brother, my natural shyness meant I was used to being alone; however, I never thought I would get into a situation where seclusion could become permanent.

Jack Hemphill

# CHAPTER TWENTY-SIX

## TRISH
## AUGUST 1952

Will noticed it first, but once he pointed it out, I became aware of the increased FBI surveillance. With the lights out in Will's apartment, I watched the men in their *invisible* cars and observed their careful rotation of agents every two hours on a twenty-four-hour basis.

"What do they expect to find?" I asked Will.

"They mostly want to know who comes to see us, where we go, and who we t-talk to. They've followed me everyplace for the last couple of weeks."

"*Why*? We're not criminals. Are they afraid of us?"

"They're not afraid of *communists*, they're afraid of *communism*. As you know, c-communism is not just a political party, or group of people, or form of government. It's a *religion*."

"So how does the FBI combat a religion?"

"That's just the p-point! It's the most difficult thing to fight because, just like religion, communism recognizes only one universal law that has absolute authority, and it isn't necessarily confined to human rationale and restrictions. Understand?"

"Not really...I'm still struggling with rational human

things, like getting you to your meeting tomorrow morning with that new senatorial candidate. I assume you don't want the FBI knowing about your connection with him."

"Right."

"What are you going to do when they follow you?"

"I've got a plan to throw them off."

"A *rational* plan?"

"I'll show you."

By 7:30 the next morning, I finished my breakfast. I left eggs, and bacon, and toast in the oven for Will, who was just getting up. With the lights out, I peeped through the curtains at the gray Ford hiding in the dark. Every half minute a red glow appeared over the steering wheel from a long drag on a cigarette by one of the agents, undoubtedly sleepy from a long, boring night of surveilling nothing. By eight, we were in the car and heading out.

"Okay, Will, what's your big plan to escape these guys?"

"Look in the mirror. You see them following about a hundred yards back?"

"Yes."

"In about two miles there will be a long straight section of road. I'll take a t-turn-off on the right, down an old dirt road. One-hundred feet down that road is a place to turn around. I'll pull in, and you and I will change places. You will complete the turnaround and drive back to the highway before they arrive at the turnoff. I'll slide down below the window line so they can't see me. When you get back to the road, turn right continuing in the same direction as we started. Watch them in the mirror. If they take the bait, which I know they will, they'll think you dropped me off somewhere in the woods. They'll consider me a more important target than you and they'll try to find me in the woods. Meanwhile, turn on highway 15 toward Pittsboro. That's where my meeting will be."

The maneuver worked exactly as he had planned and within minutes we were headed east on highway 15 with no one following us. This game continued for the next few months. I never got used to it. The FBI, who I admired and believed in my whole life, had become my predator.

# CHAPTER TWENTY-SEVEN

## TRISH
## AUGUST 1952

"You mind taking care of the door tonight," Will asked.

"How will I know who to let in?"

"Just let them in. No secret knock or anything."

"What's Francis going to talk about?"

"I don't know, but I think it'll be a fun night," he said.

The first knock on the door was Caroline Yates. I never met her, but I remembered Will warned me that she was a strong-minded and strong-willed woman. She worked in the Admission Department at Duke University and knew just about everybody in the state, including the chief aide to the governor. Caroline brought with her a stack of envelopes. Timothy Horn arrived with Francis. It seemed as if Francis was grooming him to be an upcoming star in the movement. When Francis walked in, he handed me a stack of folders and said he would give me a signal when to hand them out. As Will requested, I brought all recent or important mail for him to update everyone on current events at headquarters.

Once routine business was taken care of, Will turned the meeting over to Francis. He was dressed casually in navy-blue slacks and a starched short-sleeve white shirt, open at the collar. He stood as still as a statue in front of the crowd and said nothing until he had scanned the room and looked everyone in the eye. The room fell into dead quiet waiting for him to speak.

"I see we have our representatives from Wilmington, Charlotte, and Columbia here tonight. They've been telling me about the increased surveillance activity from the Feds outside their offices, and in two cases, at their homes. I've noticed an increase in FBI presence in Chapel Hill, and also right here at my apartment. I want to be straight with you about this, but I don't want to scare you.

"The government knows that changes are taking place in the Party; however, there is nothing to be afraid of. You people in this room are our most courageous NCCP members. That's why you are here. In spite of the assaults from Washington against communists, especially from the House Committee on Un-American Activities, I believe we have a better and more exciting future than ever before.

"As you know, the CPUSA headquarters in New York is always working on national and international issues, but the state and regional branches of the Party were told from the beginning to focus on three other areas. The first area is reeducating American youth to embrace our vision. The second area of focus is injecting socialism into every part of daily life. The third area is redefining the country's fundamental ideology and culture.

"Over the last twenty years, our largest efforts at NCCP have been focused mostly on the second goal, *socializing the daily life,* and we've done it, in part, with our efforts to redistribute wealth, especially in our factories. We're going to keep our efforts going there, but now we need to redouble our efforts on the other two areas of attack."

He picked up a booklet from the table in front of him, held it high, and said, "Let's look at the third target, *ideology*. I don't know how many of you have seen or read this report by the *Cultural Commission of the Communist Party*. It was first presented to the Fifteenth National Convention of the Party in December 1950. The report is called, *Let us Grasp the Weapon of Culture* and is being circulated by the Party all over the country in a drive to further infiltrate communism into the field of culture. In order to change the obstinate mindset of Americans, their belief systems and value systems will have to be shattered. This means a complete overhaul of all forms of creative expression. The goal is to remove all moral value in the arts and replace them with ideas that break down traditional rules and standards, preparing public thought to reject their past, which will soften their resistance to communism.

"I have a copy of the booklet for everyone, and I expect you to read it."

I looked back at will and tilted my head with a little squint in my right eye that was designed to say, *did you know he was going to talk about this?* Will raised both eyebrows and nodded slightly. I looked around the room to see if others were as shocked as I was. They all sat with their emotionless eyes fixed on Francis.

Francis said, "Now, let's look at our number-one target—*American youth and education*. We, the Party, have been working on this for a couple of decades and we've penetrated deep into institutions at all levels." He picked up another booklet from the desk and said, "This report was first printed nineteen years ago by a special committee of the *Progressive Education Association*. It is called, *A call to the Teachers of the Nation*. The *call* was a request to start a flood of discussions and articles that will lead educational circles and institutions to embrace socialism and carefully place it into every curriculum. I also have copies of this article for everyone here tonight. I want you to study it because it will give you a good background of the type of persuasion we have found effective. Today, the progressive concepts discussed in the booklet are influencing students from first-grade classes all the way through graduate schools in the most respected universities. We want children to start this training as young as possible. "

Francis walked around and sat on the corner of the table and folded his arms across his chest still holding the little booklet clutched in his hand. I think he wanted this part of his speech to look and sound personal and secret.

"We'll continue to infiltrate and influence everything that effects our children's learning. This includes the content of textbooks — especially American history, books placed in libraries, curriculum planning, librarians, teachers and teachers' unions, professors, and most of all we're continuing to infiltrate all teacher's colleges. This will ensure perpetual instruction of socialism at all levels of education."

Again, I looked around the room. I don't know what I expected or wanted to see: people stomping out, tears, faces turning red? How could I have not known about that stuff? Did everyone else in the room know about it? I thought about Betty and little Christine and other children I knew. I thought about how I would feel if I had children. I was twenty-four years old and realized I could have been a mother by then — I could have had several children by then. I wondered what I would have done for them after hearing that speech.

Francis continued, "Trish has an assignment package for each of you. Every envelope has a name on the outside with a word or two that indicates your field of work. For those of you who have packages with *Education* written on it, see Caroline Yates who is a storehouse of experience on how to infiltrate college curricula and how to approach professors as well as lower school teachers and librarians. For those who have *Medical*, *Legal*, or *religion* on your package, see Dr. Joseph Cook. For *journalists* and *culture*, come to me. After that, we'll all enjoy refreshments." He then flipped his hand, palm up, toward me which was my signal to hand out the packages and start serving coffee and cookies.

Each individual worker enthusiastically read the information put together specifically for him. After that, they formed three circles: one around Francis, one around Caroline Yates, and one around Dr. Cook. Will and I watched from the couch. I asked Will if he knew about those things. He tightened his face and nodded like he was embarrassed.

"I heard about some of these things in other parts of the country, but Why didn't I know this was going on around here? I asked.

"It was a CPUSA priority and they mostly handled it themselves with a little local support."

"Who in our group worked on it?"

"Francis and me and a few others?"

"Who else—Rebecca?"

He nodded, then said, "Francis told me from the beginning that I should never discuss those programs with you, and so he never let you read or edit correspondence that dealt with those projects."

175

"Who did it for him?"

He didn't answer at first, but the look on his face turned from embarrassment to pain.

"Answer me!" I yelled.

"Again, it was R-Rebecca," he said softly.

"But *Why*?"

"Because…they considered them national projects and he had you working only on state and regional projects."

"Why Rebecca?"

"Francis knew that when you learned about those activities, you would react *exactly* the way you did tonight."

"Why Rebecca?" I asked again.

He looked down for a moment, then said,

"Trish, to tell you the truth I've worked with her for over twenty years, very dedicated woman, but, As far as I can tell, she's the t-toughest and hardest woman I've ever met. She has neither empathy nor sympathy for anyone. That's why she's on that committee and you are not."

We watched and listened to the enthusiasm growing in the three groups for another hour. Francis announced that it was time to go home and everybody picked up their packets and left. Will and I sat on the couch for a while, but I didn't feel like talking.

...

Ever since Bearcat moved to the farm, I stopped eating my morning breakfasts on the porch at Graham Hall, but I continued my early campus walks among UNC students on their way to class. By then, I was older than most of the students. It had been years since my picture was on the front page of newspapers and almost as long since I moved my work into the back room. I wasn't surprised that nobody on campus knew me anymore.

To support the NCCP's new direction, both Francis and Will were spending less time in Chapel Hill and leaving more work for me to do. Occasionally, Will was gone a couple of weeks at a time. However, when he was in town, he sometimes stayed at the shop late at night to help with the printing. He was very kind to me, like an older brother.

Two years had gone by since I had seen Lem. Every day I imagined him coming into the store, but what would I tell him? I was still doing the things he hated so much. I constantly expected him to call. But still, I knew it would never happen. Twice a month I picked up the phone, called him, let it ring once, and hung up. I was hoping he would hear it and think about calling back or something.

For the next year, I saw less and less of Francis and Rebecca. In spite of his stern warning, I opened, read, and photographed mail addressed to Francis as soon as it came in. As instructed, I answered and forwarded other correspondence. In the middle of it all, I still had a vague hope that somewhere underneath that pile of work, there was a purpose. I guess the only thing that was clear to me then is that I had no other place to go.

Jack Hemphill

# CHAPTER TWENTY-EIGHT

## LEM
## MARCH 1953

In spite of the clear, cold air, spring green pushed its way through the ground and burst across the trees. It was Friday and Linda was closing up her store early. She had something special planned for me. She would not tell me what it was going to be. I helped her carry two sealed bags and one cardboard box to the car. Still keeping her secret, she sat beside me with a half grin on her face.

"You're gonna to make me guess, right?" I asked.

"Guess all you want, but I won't tell you even if you got it right."

"Why do I have the feelin' that I must like it – no matter what it is?"

"Because you're smart."

"True." I let it go at that, but I think it only proved that she was the smart one.

We placed everything on my kitchen counter except one bag in the refrigerator.

"The ducks sound fired up today," she said.

"I don't know why, but somethin's bothering 'em."

"Have they gotten their afternoon meal yet?"

"Yes, about an hour ago before I came for you. We

should go down and look." I pulled my rifle from the gun rack and we went out the front door, across the porch, and over the pale-green grass. Wild onions were scattered everywhere, sticking up like long green fingers. The moment the ducks saw me and Linda, they squawked even louder. "I'll walk around the first pen and you can take a look in the second," I said. Linda's face had become as familiar to them as mine and Quincy's, and I always thought they liked the sound of a woman's voice better.

"Why don't I have a rifle?" she said with a smile in her voice.

"That's because I'm smart too," I answered. Once inside, I walked the length of the right fence, then all the way down the middle, and finally back up the hill along the left fence adjacent to the pen Linda was inspecting.

"Lem, over here!" she yelled.

In less than a minute, I was beside her in the corner of the pen against the block wall. A female duck was face down with her wings spread out on the ground. She was covered in dirt and mud. When I turned her over, she made a soft cry.

"She's alive. Let's get her over to the duck hospital," I said as I slid my hands under the duck, and lifted her to my chest. The little hospital room was always warmer than the pens. Linda filled a bowl of water and collected a handful of dry rags from a shelf, and we both carefully washed the duck's body. It was not until we had washed all the dirt and mud off her face and neck that I recognized her. "Samantha!"

"Ohooo, no," Linda replied. "What happened?"

I placed Samantha on the ground feet first to see if she could stand. Her legs slid out in both directions, and she fell to one side and made no effort to right herself. Linda saw my eyes close and my head drop.

"What is it?" asked Linda

"She was attacked."

"Oh, God!" Linda delicately stroked Samantha's head and neck. "Was it a predator or a duck?"

"Another duck, otherwise she would be gone." I wanted to cry, but Linda beat me to it. We couldn't talk as we continued to wash her down and place her in a straw nest prepared for her against the back wall.

"All we can do now is see if she makes it through the night," I said.

"Can we remake her nest back in the mudroom?"

"Sure."

I watched her periodically all night. I could tell she saw me, and I know she heard me talking to her as I stroked her head, but she did not respond any more than that. Early in the morning, before Linda arrived, I took Samantha back to the duck hospital and put her in a submersion tub. Her head sank under and she couldn't straighten herself enough to pull her head out of the water. This was one of the first things I always looked for in a wounded duck because ducks have to submerge their heads regularly to clean the nostril holes in their beak. This is necessary for them to breathe properly. If they can't do it, they die.

I had already called Quincy to come a little early that morning. I carried Samantha under my left arm and held her head up with my right hand. I placed her carefully over the barrel behind the barn and gently laid her head in line with her neck. Quincy waited while I stroked her head and talked to her. After a few minutes, I stepped back and nodded to Quincy, but Samantha, somehow, found the strength to straighten her neck and raise her head higher than her wings. She turned to look at me. Neither Quincy nor I moved or said a word, just watched her. After about a half minute, her head started bobbing lower and lower until it rested again on the barrel. We waited for another minute and there was no change. I nodded again to Quincy, who placed the edge of his hatchet across the back of her head, then slowly raised it high.

"Quincy, wait!" I said as I threw both hands in the air. I walked back to Samantha, lifted her head, and looked into her eyes. "Not yet," I said softly. Quincy nodded and walked to the shed to put away his hatchet.

Linda was waiting for me by the pens. With Samantha in my arms, we walked together back to the house. I laid the duck between Linda and me as we sat on hay still scattered on the mudroom floor. Samantha raised her little white head a few inches just long enough to see we were there. She then rested on the soft straw. The next day, she continued to lift her head periodically, but took no water or food. The following day was exactly the same. We both spent time talking to her. By the third day she took some water and from there started a slow but steady recovery. After a few weeks, with tiny duck steps, she was able to waddle slowly to the pens and even slower back to the house. From that day on, we never let her go back to the pens, and she slept and took her food in the mudroom. During the day, she still insisted on following me around the yard to supervise my chores.

# CHAPTER TWENTY-NINE

## TRISH
## MAY 1953

Empty houses echo. That was my first thought when we walked into Betty's house.

Betty and her oldest daughter sat on a suitcase and a wooden crate in the living room. That was the first chance Will and I had to see her since we heard the mill was closing.

"Betty," I said as I walked toward her. She looked up for one moment and flashed an embarrassed smile that vanished immediately. She started to say something, but her lips quivered slightly and she dropped her head.

"Betty, I'm so sorry this happened. How are your children taking this?"

"She nodded, took a deep breath and said, "Some goin' to stay with my mother, some with my brother. I'm goin' to look for another job in another mill, probably closer to Greensboro. I got a place to stay down there."

"Is somebody coming to get you?"

"Yes, my brother. He got my other kids earlier."

"How often will you get to see your children?" I asked.

"Only every few weeks."

"Oh, Betty . . ." I started crying and turned away to hide

my face. Everything was gone. Every stick of furniture, every belonging except one large canvas bag with the image of flowers stitched on the side.

Half the houses in the village appeared empty. There is something about empty houses. A feeling like something big was left behind by the family that lived there. Perhaps their lingering thoughts.

Only one month before then, on the first day of the week, the mill gave one short message to all workers and employees informing them that the mill was permanently suspending operations at the end of the day on the following Friday.

"After all that work, after the conditions got so much better — how could they close it down?" I asked.

Betty whispered, "They said in their message that they couldn't afford it no more,"

"That's it?"

"That's all they said, but I talked to the labor foreman, who told me the plant couldn't afford to buy all the new equipment they needed for all them new synthetic fibers commin' out now, and at the same time keep up with all our new demands."

"Synthetic fibers?"

"Yes, I already knew about nylon, but he told me they got something called *rayon,* and something else. I think they called it *acrylic wool,* and they didn't have no more money to get all that new equipment and stuff they needed to compete."

"You mean that's all they said without any other warning? They just called it quits?"

"I guess maybe they did warn us a couple of times, but I told you 'bout it, and don't you remember? You didn't believe it."

I looked at Will. She was right. We didn't believe what the mill was saying. We thought it was nothing more than smoke; a way to put the workers back in their place, so the owners could continue to enjoy the profits at Betty and the other worker's expense. "Are they going to sell it or something, or open it later?"

"Nope. I looked into their offices. They were gone, and all files, their pictures, and personal things were gone."

I wanted to comfort her somehow. I wanted to hug her. I wanted to tell her it was going to be okay, but all we could do was say we were sorry about what happened. I kissed her goodbye and told her to keep in touch because I was interested in her. She said she would; however, we both knew we would never see each other or hear from each other again.

# CHAPTER THIRTY

## WILL
## JUNE 1953

The Korean War finally stopped; however, I had no time to celebrate.

The FBI was still keeping track of me, and I enjoyed driving them crazy. I finally figured out my phone had been tapped. I didn't know how long. My new green Plymouth was easy to spot and easy to follow; so, secretly, I bought another car. One of our workers had an uncle who sold me a car that had been parked in his backyard for a couple of years. I gave a cashier's check to the nephew for the car and a license plate that had never been used. He delivered it to the parking lot behind the store where my green Plymouth was parked. I left the keys to the Plymouth on Trish's desk with a note that said she could have the Plymouth if she wanted it.

Early Sunday morning, I took off in my Ford, painted the same color gray as all the FBI cars. Driving from Chapel Hill to Winston Salem, I managed to be FBI free, but the moment I turned onto the street where I grew up, and where my mother still lived, I saw another gray Ford parked not fifty yards down the street near the long driveway to my family's house. I parked in a church lot at the end of the block, then I walked behind the church through a strip of woods that extended all the way past the rear of Mom's house. I entered through her back door. Mom was cooking herself breakfast in the kitchen. She was startled but thrilled to see me, and, as all mothers do, her first words scolded me for not coming to see her at Christmas.

"Good to see you Mom," I said, "You look g-good." It was a white lie. She had aged since the last time I had been home, and I'm sure Mom didn't understand why. I could tell Dad's death had been hard on her. I took some comfort in the fact that my brother lived only a mile down the road and took care of her. He was, however, not any more forgiving of me than Dad had been.

"I'm not going to be able to stay, Mom."

"Can you be here with me just one day?"

"Mom I…" I started to tell her that I was going to be in hiding for a long time, and she may not see me again, but she was so much weaker than I expected I changed direction and said, "Okay, but I'll have to leave very early in the morning."

"I'll make you a good breakfast."

"No, Mom. Just coffee in the morning, but I'll help you with lunch today and we'll make a good dinner together tonight." Mom believed my long separation from her was over and spoke as if I would be coming to see her often, but there was a good chance I would go to prison.

The next morning, when I kissed her goodbye, I looked into her eyes, and I memorized every line on her kind and loving face, in case that was the last time I would see her. I knew if I was sent to prison, Mom would die of sorrow. I'm glad I took the risk to visit that day. She lived another four months before dying in her sleep.

Slipping out in the morning before sunrise was easy, and again I was FBI free during my trip around the state. My last stop was at a branch office, above the Dilworth Barber Shop at the corner of an old suburb close to downtown Charlotte. I arranged for one of our workers to meet me a block away from the shop and drive me in my gray car to a safe place, in thick woods, beside the Catawba River. I told him if I was arrested, he could keep the car, but until then, be ready to pick me up at any moment.

From the little cabin, I managed to talk to Trish on the phone. To keep from being traced, I limited the phone calls to thirty seconds at a time. I instructed her to write paychecks for herself and the other employees every two weeks. Trish said two men in a car with long antennas were always parked near the store, and they were still at my apartment every night. I told her she should look for a good hiding place nobody knows about, not even her own family.

I missed Trish more than anything else.

# CHAPTER THIRTY-ONE

## TRISH
### JULY 1953

I never got used to being watched and followed wherever I went. It made no sense because I wasn't somebody important like Will or Francis. Will was gone, and as far as we knew, he was gone forever. At random times, he made very short phone calls to me. Although I never knew where he was, he sent monthly checks to pay the apartment rent. I drove his car to work almost every day, even though it was a marked vehicle, but so was mine.

For the last few years, I had been delivering packages to a contact in Raleigh. Francis had set it all up, and my job was to find ways to evade the FBI. Under no circumstance was I to be caught, or even seen, handing over the packages to the contact. So I constantly looked for ways to escape the gray men that were bird-dogging me all the time. The number one thing I learned was to never be predictable.

Other than my trips to Raleigh and occasional trips to the mills, my job was very routine, consisting of printing, writing, and mailing. I didn't know what the FBI was expecting to find by watching and tailing me for so long. After a while, I couldn't contain my growing fear of what they would do to me if they arrested me. I didn't want to hide like a hunted animal, and I couldn't go back to the farm. I still had no place to go other than the bookstore and Will's apartment.

Francis was gone. All of the accounting and bookkeeping for the shop, as well as the business management, had always been done by an independent group. Most of that work was done by a quiet little man who came in monthly, took care of business, and left with few comments.

Jackie was off that day, and Carole and I held down the shop. No other party members came in. About once an hour, Carole walked to the front display windows and leaned forward far enough to check on the surveillance team which was constantly watching us. She seldom talked much about politics or communism probably because I never talked about it. We both felt very much alone—almost like decoys floating in a pond. We were never told half of what was going on, and with Will hiding somewhere and Francis out of sight, we needed to protect ourselves. I never told Carole that since Will left, a team of agents had been following me and were still watching Will's apartment at night. I finally concluded that if they suspected Will enough to watch him day and night, they would also be suspicious of the woman he worked with, and who lived in his apartment. I had a feeling they believed things about me and my position with the party that weren't true.

After several hours of sorting mail and filing, I stepped into the front sales area for a little break. Carole called me to the counter. She had a strange look on her face. "Trish," she said, "walk over to the window. Look across Franklin Street and tell me what you see."

"What are you talking about?"

"Just look normal and do it. Okay?" I squinted at her slightly and walked to the window on the right side of the front door. I saw the gray car, off to the left, parked in his usual spot. I looked across the street toward the old well at the far end of the campus. Students were scurrying around like schools of fish in a pond. An older man, who looked like a professor, was contemplating his feet as he plodded along the sidewalk on the other side of Franklin Street. Then I saw the obvious and couldn't believe I didn't notice it immediately. Directly in front of the old professor, was another gray car with oversized radio antennas and two men sitting in the front seat watching me.

"What do you think this means?" asked Carole.

"I don't know but let me see if I can get Francis on the phone."

"Good luck," said Carole. "I dialed his number four times this morning and no answer."

"I think we should start cleaning up and gathering our things."

It was Wednesday, and my normal day to make bank deposits was Thursday. I hoped the men who had been watching us for weeks wouldn't notice the small change in my routine. As I walked up the sidewalk, I smiled at the men in the car. As usual, they pretended not to see me. I went straight to the bank and closed out all of the accounts for The North Carolina Communist Party and withdrew all the money in cash.

I returned to the back room, unlocked the file drawers, and removed all the correspondence files, all the photograph files, and the metal lockbox. I placed the documents in the army knapsack that Lem gave me for my birthday. I had been using it mostly to carry my breakfast and lunch, along with a few personal items; however, it was a perfect container for all of the files, forms, pictures, and documents of bank transactions. I stuffed the cash in the lockbox.

By midafternoon, I slipped out the back door and placed the backpack in the trunk of Will's green car along with the steel lockbox. As far as I could tell, no one saw me go out to the car, or return to the shop, not even Carole.

A little before four o'clock I said to Carole, "Let's lock up. The car's out back and I'll give you a ride home without going down Franklin Street. That way they won't even notice we're gone."

"I'll be ready in five minutes," she said.

We never knew how long it took the four men to figure out that we were gone, but Carole and I smiled for the first time in weeks. I dropped her off at her place and said goodbye like it might be the last time we would ever see each other again.

Instead of heading south to Will's apartment, I drove north toward the mill in Durham to take care of some final business up there that only I could do. Then I drove back toward the apartment. The closer I got to Chapel Hill, the more uneasy I felt. Everything that happened that day filled my mind and piled on top of the stress accumulated over the last few months. Why were there four men watching us? Where were Will, and Francis, and everybody else in the Party who we worked with and constantly called us on the phone, and wrote us letters, and came into the store?

I couldn't return to the apartment, or the store, or to my farm.

I missed my brother, my best friend, but I did not want

to get him involved in my mess. Before Lem threw me out, everything was easy. I never feared anything when Lem was near, but now I was afraid of everything—afraid in ways I never thought about before. I was also ashamed, not because of what my friends back home must have thought, but what Lem must have thought.

Chapel Hill, familiar buildings, houses, bends in the old road—all the things I had seen a thousand times—flashed by me as I drove without knowing where I was going. I was on Chicken Bridge Road approaching the turnoff to my farm. Like everything else, my driveway floated silently by me. The turnoff to the old Honeycutt farm was Just beyond. I remembered the farm had been abandoned, and so I turned into the long curving drive. The old house had fallen in, but the barn was still standing. The large barn doors were big enough to drive the car inside. I closed them behind me and latched the floor bolts. That barn would become my cocoon and I was finally isolated from everything.

Jack Hemphill

# CHAPTER THIRTY-TWO

## LEM
### AUGUST 1953

Bearcat took great pride in his home and in his occupation as chief guard of the ducks. He knew all sounds, both day and night, and never let any unfamiliar noise go by without a bark, a growl, and an inspection. Twice he caught foxes trying to dig under the fence, and he chased them away. Regularly he ran to the edge of the woods to scare off things he smelled or heard. During my morning routine, he followed me and helped me inspect everything.

Quincy was my only human companion during the week, and on the weekend, I always looked forward to Linda coming to help and be with me.

After Trish left, I never looked into her room. I couldn't stand the thought that she was lured into something against everything that she, and I, and the family believed in. She was still the most precious person I had ever known, and suddenly she was gone. It felt like she had died. She would never come back on her own, and even if she did, I was afraid she wouldn't be the same. I could never accept her. I struggled with the fact that I had thrown her out.

After all the duckies had their breakfast and their fill of

water, I let them go into the yard. Bearcat walked behind me back to the house. When we reached the top of the hill, Bearcat trotted to the spot where he watched over the flock going about their morning routine.

All noises are exaggerated when you are alone. The springs of my couch cried out louder than usual as I stretched across it. Trish's scarf was still on the coffee table where she left it. I thought of nothing for a while, but that moment of peace didn't last. I gave her that scarf almost ten years earlier. She never bought another one. It wasn't her favorite color and didn't match her eyes or the color of her hair. But I knew she liked it only because it came from me. I should have given her another one. I listened to the springs complain again as I rolled into a standing position, walked to her room, and placed the scarf on her bureau. Her bed was still unmade. I was surprised to see how many things she left behind—things she loved and things she would need. Most of her books were still neatly stacked in shelves by her bed. Her closet door was left open.

Bearcat started barking. I walked to the end of the porch and saw two men in the driveway, stepping out of a car.

"Are you Lem Basil?" asked one of the men.

"Yes, that's me. Who are you?" I walked closer. Each of the two men flashed their badge at me.

"We're FBI agents. Are you the brother of Patricia Basil?"

"Yes, but she moved out a long time ago. I don't know where she is now."

"Has she tried to contact you?"

"No, we aren't close."

"Do you know a man named Will Logan?"

"Met him once, years ago. Haven't seen him since. Tell me what's this about."

"May we come in?"

"Will you tell me what this is about?"

"I think we need to go inside."

I looked at them both. They stood still, like two blocks of granite. "Okay," I said and looked down to be sure Bearcat, who had stalked his way to my side, understood that the men were friendly.

Both sides of my couch, squeaked as the two agents sat down at each end, and placed their hats on the center cushion. I pulled a straight back chair from the dining area and sat directly in front of them. They actually waited for me to speak. "Now, will you please tell me what this is all about?"

"Are you aware that your sister and the man she lives with, Will Logan, are members of the Communist Party?"

I placed both fists on my knees, leaned forward, and said, "I knew *he* was workin' with the Party, but I don't think she was a member. *Trisha* would never join that sort of thing! And I didn't know she was livin' with that Logan guy."

"Well, Mr. Basil, are you aware that your sister has been a principal player in the coordination of Party activity for the last few years."

I folded my arms across my chest and leaned back in the chair. I was certain they were mistaken.

"She's been workin' in the bookstore in Chapel Hill for a number of years. She's very smart and literary, and all that stuff and they knew it, and that's why they hired her." The two men returned an expressionless stare. I took a deep breath to keep myself calm, then continued, "She told me she just does her job there in the bookstore, and they do their Party business in the back. She told me she *never joined*, never got involved with it—that communism stuff. I saw the article in the papers and her picture with the others, and we got into a big argument about it, and that's the reason why she left, but…"

One of the agents cut me off and said, "We have a list of the members of the Communist Party of North Carolina and she's been on that list for a least four years."

"Who put together that list?"

"We did."

"Well, you made a mistake. Where did you get the information?"

"We compiled it from many sources."

The second agent said, "In addition to that, Mr. Basil, she has signed hundreds of letters and documents for the Party. She has also been photographed in Party rallies and demonstrations all around this part of the state."

"But she wouldn't get into it that deep. She's never been political. She's just a damn *do-gooder*."

"She, and Will Logan, and a close colleague named Francis Schoberg are three of the four top Party workers in the state, and all four have gone missing."

"*What?*" I screamed. I jumped to my feet. Bearcat heard me yell and scratched at the front door and let out the loudest bark I had ever heard. I opened the door and let him in, not so much for protection, but to distract me and give me time to think what I should say next. I sat on the edge of the chair, and all I could say was, "I don't know anything about that stuff?"

"Allow us to look at her room."

"Do you have one of those…?"

"No, we don't have a search warrant, but if you need to see one, we'll be back here within two hours with a warrant to search everything in the house. For now, we just want to look into her room."

I stood and motioned for them to follow. Systematically they started on opposite sides of the room and looked over, under, and inside everything, even all items in the dirty clothes basket. One of the agents wrote down the name of every book on her shelf, including the Bible.

"What are you goin' to do when… I mean, *if* you find her?"

"Take her in for questioning."

"'Take her in? What the *hell* does that mean? Has she broken any laws?"

"If she is a member of the Communist Party, she has."

"But what do you think she's done wrong?"

"We told you a little while ago there is substantial evidence that she is a member of the North Carolina Party and the National Communist Party. Believe me, it would be in her best interest if we found her very soon."

"Will you let me know when you find her?"

"I can't promise that Mr. Basil, but we'd like for you to call us if she notifies you." One of them handed me his card.

I didn't answer. I just let them leave. I then walked back and slammed shut her bedroom door.

Jack Hemphill

# CHAPTER THIRTY-THREE

## TRISH
## OCTOBER 1953

Every day, through the hayloft window in the old Honeycutt barn, I looked out at my family farm. My house must have been four hundred yards away, but I had a good view of the house including Lem's truck and part of the drive. The Honeycutt farm had been vacant for years and you couldn't see the barn from any road, so it was a perfect hideout. Of course, I didn't know how long I would be there. Even though the barn was drafty, I was out of the rain and no one could see me. At first, I slept in the back seat of the car. It felt safe, but it wasn't warm. The hayloft still had dozens of tightly packed bales, and I stacked them high on the loft floor like children's wooden blocks forming a tunnel with a little sleeping nest inside. It was warm and soft, and by using a large bale to close off the mouth of the tunnel, I felt completely safe where no one could ever find me. In another little compartment inside the nest, I hid my knapsack, metal lockbox, and other items.

The old Honeycutt farmhouse was gone, but the well was near the barn. After a little priming and a lot of pumping, I was able to draw as much fresh water every day as I would ever need. Because I could see Lem's truck from the loft window, I knew when he was gone. So two or three times a week I slipped over to my house to steal food, and some clothing, and help myself to duck eggs. The number of things I took was always small enough so Lem wouldn't notice. Of course, the first time I stepped into the yard, Bearcat barked and ran at me. As soon as he recognized me, he was instantly my good buddy again. I always found some scraps of meat in the refrigerator for him. I also took from the house a box of matches and a small pan.

I made a pile of rocks in a circle on the dirt floor of the Honeycutt Barn, directly below the hay loft window. In the middle of my rock pile, I created a small burn pit to cook my eggs with occasional berries found around the farm. I always opened the hayloft window, just a little, high above the burn pit to let the smoke out.

I still had very little to eat and almost nothing to do. So in addition to stealing food, I started borrowing from the stack of books in my bedroom at the farm, taking one or two per week and replacing them on following trips. The only other things I read were the documents I took from the file drawers at the bookstore. I reread all the letters and documents slowly, pausing to be sure I absorbed everything that was sent out, and every reply that came back. I had many weeks to think about all the different people in my life. And I had time to think about myself.

I pictured Will as a stray cat, helplessly loyal to whoever fed him first.

I saw Francis as nothing more than a hound dog forever chasing rabbits he would never catch, but he was so determined, he forgot about everything and everybody else.

I finally saw myself as a book, with the top half of every page filled with my most personal scribblings, and the bottom half filled in by everyone who ever knew me.

As always, I saw Lem as my perpetual big brother — my own personal giant.

The nights were growing colder, and it was hard to keep track of the days. The only time I ventured out of the barn was to get water at night and during the day when Lem was gone. I needed more food. My slacks and blouse felt loose on my body and I started sleeping a little longer each day. Enough light came through the window in the loft for me to lie down in the straw, beside my hay hut, read, and watch for Lem to leave. Whenever he did, I dropped my book and dashed toward the house as fast as I could.

Both ponds on our farm were fed by artesian springs that oozed out of the side of the hill and created a long marsh area flowing into the ponds. There was once an easy path from the Honeycutt barn to our farm, but because of the rising water table over the last few years, the marsh had expanded into the thick woods. I had to walk almost to our driveway, and then loop around the top of the spring. Once I got around the wetlands, I walked back down the hill on the opposite bank near the duck pens. I did this to be sure I was always out of sight.

One afternoon, I saw a car hidden behind a thicket of low bushes. A man was sitting in the front seat watching the house. I waited an hour. He didn't move. After a while, Lem returned and nodded to the man who continued to watch. Evening came and the forest grew dark, then the sky turned black. Lights turned on in the house. The car's red brake lights lit up then went off as his rear lights came on. The car backed out of his hiding place without turning on his headlights. Thinking he was leaving, I started inching my way toward the drive, when another car, without lights on, and making almost no sound, nestled into the same hiding place behind the thicket. Except for the tiny glow of a cigarette, I couldn't see the car at all. Twenty-four-hour surveillance continued from then on.

It was a wet fall and most of the rain fell in the late afternoon or at night. The barn had a tin roof, partly rusted, but only a few leaks. Rain on the roof sounded like a thousand tiny drums in perfect rhythm. I can't remember ever feeling safer than I did on those rainy nights, in my straw cave, inside total darkness, with the roof's relentless roar. I slept so soundly, that it felt like I would never wake. Those hours gave me the only relief I could get from the pain of nagging hunger.

One day at dusk, in mid-October, I saw Lem drive away. By the time I climbed halfway up the hill, I was exhausted. I had eaten almost nothing for the past week. I trudged close to the driveway. The car was there, watching my house.

My options were shrinking. I couldn't turn myself in. They would find out I had been living next door all along, and they would accuse Lem of hiding me. I could drive away and find another hiding place, but I still wouldn't have food. Again I remembered how totally isolated I was, and that I had no place to go. If the FBI was willing to put a constant surveillance on my house, then they were probably looking for me everywhere.

I was starving and desperate. What to do next was no longer a thinking thing. I had to do whatever it took. I knew there was enough duck feed scattered around the floor of the duck pens to glean a meal each night. The only option left was to sneak by the FBI car in the dark, quietly gather the food from the trough and floor of the pens, sneak back to the barn, and survive another day. It only took minutes to make a fire in the pit and boil enough water to make mush out of the feed. That was probably the only way I could make the mush go down and stay down. I had an old tin cup in the barn to scoop up grain. The straw on the pen floor made a good place to sit with my back against the stone wall and sometimes take a short rest.

Back at the barn, the meager meal satisfied me enough to sleep, but the following morning I knew I was still starving, and I knew I was growing weaker.

October became November. I had learned to walk silently through the woods and thickets. I realized I had become one of the night animals, a predator sliding secretly into the duck pens, stealing my daily meal, and disappearing back through the woods. Each time I went, I had one motive – kill the hunger for one more day. The Moon was the only light, and it was just bright enough to see a spider web fixed in the corner between the wood post and the stone wall. I had been gone so long from the farm that none of the ducks knew me, and they ran away as I walked through the pen. In the corner, three or four drakes stretched their necks as they vigorously pecked at the hundreds of newly hatched spiders scrambling over the edges of the web. For every spider eaten by the ducks, at least twenty slipped away, through the fence, under the straw, and into the dark. I was tired and decided to rest for a while before going back to the barn. How long I slept, I don't know. I felt something moving slowly over my foot, and I jumped and instinctively slapped my leg. I felt the cold unmistakable sting of sharp fangs sinking into my right calf. I screamed so loud the entire flock in every pen roared with hundreds of deafening squawks. I jumped to my feet and hobbled toward the door. The snake hung from my leg with its fangs still engaged. With my left hand, I grabbed him behind his head and threw him to the ground. He immediately slithered a couple of feet away from me before sliding under the thick hay, out of sight. My leg was becoming numb as I ran through the gate and started up the hill. The agent undoubtedly heard the commotion and was already sweeping the path beside the marsh with a flashlight that struck my eyes, momentarily blinding me.

"Stop right there!" he yelled.

I turned toward a cluster of cattails in the marsh. My only instinct was to bolt into whatever seemed to give some kind of protection. I still don't know why I went into the marsh except I thought it was an obstacle the man wouldn't cross. The marsh was wider and deeper than I ever remembered it. Within seconds, I was up to my thighs in muck and sinking faster. I turned back toward the bank. The numbness in my right leg and foot turned to flaming pain. I couldn't move. I fell face forward into mud over my head, and I couldn't push myself up. My legs were stuck. Thrashing back and forth I sank deeper. Fear struck me so hard, I froze.

I felt the agents' meaty hands grab my back and drag me out of the water onto the bank. He rolled me over to see if I was breathing. I coughed and spit muck out of my mouth.

"Are you alright?" he yelled.

I screamed — no words, just animal sounds.

"I'll assume that's a *yes*," he said, then continued, "Well, you're under arrest." He rolled me over to put handcuffs on me, but the pain pushed out another scream.

"Snake b…!" was all I could say.

He pulled me to my feet and held me up by the back of my coat as we walked to his car. I dragged my right leg, and I was totally covered in black stinking mud, muck, and mush. His hands, and legs, and much of his front side were coated black. He cuffed my left hand to a strap in the back seat and locked the doors. By the time he turned his car around, Lem was standing in the driveway holding a rifle. The agent pulled in front of him, rolled his window partially down and said, "Step out of the way."

Lem cupped his hands against the back window to see who had been arrested. I looked up at him. My eyelids were so caked with clay they barely opened. My nose, ears, and hair were sculpted into a mud form so different from my normal face, that he couldn't possibly recognize me. He stepped back. The agent immediately sped away.

Jack Hemphill

# CHAPTER THIRTY-FOUR

## WILL
## DECEMBER 1953

I had not talked nor seen another person in a long time. I was actually startled when I heard a knock on the door. I pushed my lips against the crack between the door and the frame, and said, using the most intimidating voice I could throw out, "Who's th-there?"

"Will, open the damn door. It's Francis," he said, pretending to be annoyed.

I unlocked the deadbolt and the door latch. Francis was leaning against one of the posts on the porch.

"Glad to see you're still alive," he said.

"Glad to hear you say that. I wasn't sure if I was. Come on in." Once inside, I locked the door behind us.

"Why are you here?" I asked.

"I'm heading to a hideout in South Carolina."

"If the Feds are after you, going over the state line w-won't...it won't help."

"I got friends down there. I can hide indefinitely."

"Is that what you want?"

"Doesn't matter."

"Well, it does to me. I'm going *nuts* like this!"

"Make me a big cup of coffee while I use your

bathroom," he commanded.

I was waiting at the kitchen table with two cups of steaming coffee, and a leftover biscuit when he said, "What the hell's that?"

"My last biscuit."

"Christ, Will... you got jam?"

"Nope, but there's a market about ten miles from here."

"You get your supplies there?"

"God, no, I don't leave this house — ever. I got someone to make weekly deliveries. The biscuit's yours if you want it; if not, it goes back into the frig...You want it?"

"Let me tell you where the Party's going," he said, without answering my question. He left the biscuit on the table until he finished half of his coffee, then he broke the biscuit in two and dunked part of it into his brew, bit off the sopped side, and continued talking. "I'll bet you think it's over."

"Don't you?" I replied with a flat voice.

"No. We're in a transitional stage."

"What are you t-talking about? You...you're on the run, I'm in hiding. God only knows where Trish is by now. Between the FBI and Joe McCarthy, we're all but extinct. D-don't...don't you know that?"

"The transition's been going on for a long time."

"*Transition*? Into what? We've got no place to go!"

"Ahh, my friend, ask yourself why after three decades, we've captured so few American minds."

"I don't know, but what's that got to do with anything?"

"It was always so simple, and we didn't know it. Just a slow constant guiding of public thought, that's all we needed. We never had to mention communism. Picture this...if we get Americans to believe a *new, or better way*

212

of thinking is coming from their *own* deep beliefs, they'll stand up and fight for it. They won't even realize it came from us."

"I can't think of anything that's happened over the years that would make you, or me, or anybody s-so optimistic. Where's all of that c-coming from?"

"Our only mistake over the last thirty years was believing we could march across this country and bully our way into a soft spot somewhere in the American mind. You're right about McCarthy and the FBI. They turned that mind against us. But McCarthy, without knowing it, has given us a great gift—one we could never achieve ourselves.

"McCarthy? A gift?"

"He, unwittingly, turned his anticommunist alarm bell into a national disgrace. Future Americans will look back and laugh at what they'll call *commie phobia*, and they'll never again take rumors or reports against communism seriously.

"Okay Francis, I'll pretend you're right, but you never explained the *transition* you mentioned."

"*The great red fear*, which we saw popping up all over the country, will no longer be an obstacle to Americans. Their preconceptions of communism will vanish with time. New perspectives will sprout, containing the concepts we've supported and planted all along, but in new, more acceptable, forms. As that happens, some objections to it will rise again, but the objections will go nowhere because nobody wants to be labeled *commie phobic*. They'll be overwhelmed by the fresh and beautiful forms of socialism, now seeping into everyone's life, like a long-overdue medication."

"I hope you're right, Francis, but I don't know where all the things we've started in the p-past are going."

"The past will continue to do whatever it's supposed to do. I *now* see myself becoming a different person, and Francis Schoberg will cease to exist."

"What does that mean?"

"Will, you and I have reached a point where our paths are going in different directions."

"I know. It's been going on for a couple of years."

"And what have you noticed?"

"I continued to do the things I've always done for the Party, and you've b-been slowly disappearing."

"Yes, you're very loyal. That's your great asset and you'll stick with it to the end."

"And you understand that the *end* is near, right?" I said.

"Actually, that takes us back to the *transition*."

"Okay, the one you never explained."

"I don't think I really have to explain it," he said.

"Because we are in hiding?"

"No… well, partly."

"Because there's no way the Party is going to be the same again?"

"Yes, that's right," he said.

"And you'll v-vanish?"

"Gone."

"And I'll be caught, and tried, and sent to p-prison, and when I get out, I'll be b-branded for l-life?"

"Yes, you and lots of other loyal workers," he paused, "that's the transition." He paused again. "Part of the Party will disappear from view like me. But the remnant, the part that is still visible, like you and many others, will serve a great purpose."

"You mean like me and Trish?

"Yes! You and Trish and lots of others. Americans need to see the communists rounded up and punished. They need to see people get arrested, convicted, and sent away for a long time. Then the people will stop fearing communists, let go, and that fear will never come back no matter what happens."

I understood what he was implying, and I understood what he meant by *disappear* and *remnant*. I looked at him in silence, holding back a flow of emotion and pure rage.

Francis, reading my face, said, "I know how hard this is for you to take right now all at once, but I believe you'll honor your oath to the Party, and you've already made a significant contribution to its growth—it may even be a higher contribution than mine, certainly more unselfish. We have this in common: our lives are over as we knew them, but of course, our lives are nothing, compared to what we're accomplishing."

I got up and threw the rest of my coffee into the sink. It splashed up the wall a couple of feet.

"What the hell is wrong?" he yelled.

"You!" I yelled back.

"Cool down Will. Didn't you just hear what I said? We're doing all the right things. It's still a great time to be a communist."

"I've finally figured you out—either you're *nuts*, or you've sold me out."

"Of course not."

"I'm not worth *squat* to you, am I?"

"That's ridiculous. I've just said you've done great things for the Party."

215

"And what if I don't continue doing *great things and what if I stop supporting the cause*?"

"Then...I guess you wouldn't be worth *squat*, Will."

I must have known he thought that way all along. I breathed in deeply and slowly let it out, then said, "We're not animals, Francis."

"Our only worth was our service to the cause. I thought you knew that better than anybody." Francis sat still and contemplated his coffee, while I wiped down the wall. After that, I stared out the window at the red Catawba River flowing by the cabin, then asked, "Where are you going from here?"

"First, I'm going ten miles down the road to that store you told me about and find a sandwich; then I'm going to melt into the faceless crowd of Carolina soybean farmers."

"You think you're going to pass as a Carolina soybean farmer? Good luck."

"Don't worry about me, I've got lots of help."

"Communists?

"No, yes, well some of them."

"Then who are they?"

"There are lots of people around with no affiliation with any party, who think the way we do and are eager to help."

"Well, like I said, good luck."

He extended his hand to say a final goodbye. I hesitated, shoved both hands into my pockets, then said, "Goodbye Francis." He turned, never looked back, and was gone.

One of the things I cherished growing up was silence. Silence was a place where my mind felt like it could expand forever. But at that moment silence was all I had left, it covered me like a thick blanket and it was suffocating me.

I sat still at my kitchen table until the sun went down. The Party, my family, and God had all gone away, and I didn't know where.

I wrote a note to the grocery delivery boy, instructing him to cancel my account in two weeks. I knew exactly what to do. All decisions had been made for me, and suddenly I was glad it was almost over.

Jack Hemphill

# CHAPTER THIRTY-FIVE

## WILL
## JANUARY 1954

My Charlotte contact picked me up. I had owned the Ford only a short time, but it felt good to be riding in it again, to be close to something familiar. I felt no need to delay or hurry, but I was resigned to let the past meet the future and accept whatever they had mapped out for me. The Catawba River and the forest gave way to radio towers, drive-in movies, car dealers, grocery stores, barbershops, and neighborhoods.

Highway 49 became Tryon Street, and downtown Charlotte stood in front of me like stone and brick boxes thirteen stories tall. I managed to find Trade Street and the Federal Building with its adjacent parking lot. After thanking my driver, and a goodbye pat on the roof of my car, I entered the building. A door at the end of a long corridor said, in small black letters, *Federal Bureau of Investigation*.

I stepped into a reception area with a counter separating me from three secretaries banging away on their typewriters. With two folders tucked tightly under my arm, I waited until one of the women came to the counter and said, "Yes?"

Without hesitation, I spit out the only thing I had practiced, "My name is William Logan. I believe you are looking for me and I want to talk to an agent."

She crinkled her brow and looked me over, then said, "*You're* William Logan?" The look on her face and the tone in her voice implied what she was actually thinking: *You're such a small, insignificant, humble looking person. How could you be the William Logan wanted by the FBI?* I refused to answer her stupid question. She took two steps back, turned, and walked to a side door, stopped, glanced back at me to be sure I had not jumped over the counter. The two other secretaries stopped typing. They were both glaring at me with their fingertips still on the typewriter keys. As soon as I looked back at them, they turned their gaze back to their motionless fingers hoping I hadn't noticed they were gawking. Before that moment, I never connected the idea of *fear* to the concept of *respect*. For three seconds, I felt significant, purposeful, accomplished, memorable, and dangerous enough to be respected.

But that feeling vanished when another door opened beside me, and two men wearing suits and no smiles surrounded me. One stepped behind me, one walked close to my side and led the way back through the door and down a corridor. I was escorted into a large room with a plain table in the center just big enough for three seats on each of the two long sides. I clutched my two folders against my chest. The four walls were blank except for a large mirror built into the wall I was facing. I was seated on one side of the table, and the larger of the two agents sat opposite me. The other agent remained standing.

The man sitting across from me took the lead by saying "I'm Agent Waters, standing behind me is Agent Lemay.

I understand you have introduced yourself as William Logan, is that right?"

"I introduced myself as *William Logan, and I believe you are looking for me.*"

"Good. We're going to ask you some questions." Agent Lemay placed a stack of manila folders in the center of the table. I still kept my folders clutched close to my chest. Agent Lemay thumbed through his stack until he found one that he placed in front of Agent Waters. It had my name on it, *William Albert Logan.* I hadn't seen my middle name written for years. Thought it had been forgotten. When he opened the folder, I noticed paper clips on certain pages, and red lines scratched under many statements.

Agent Waters looked over his shoulder and nodded to Agent Lemay who then unlocked and opened the door and let a third agent walk in. I didn't pay much attention to him. He was dressed like the other two, wore the same haircut and walked with the same FBI Swagger.

"William Logan, this is Agent Hill," said Waters.

I nodded at him without even glancing in his direction, and he returned the greeting by saying, *"Hello, Will,"* in a voice so familiar I had to look. I couldn't believe the face staring back at me. *"Horn? Tim Horn?"* I blurted out. "What the *hell* are you d-doing here?"

"I think they just told you. I'm an FBI Agent."

I closed my eyes as hard as I could, then opened them again. "You're a *mole*?

"Ten years with the Bureau."

*"Sonofabitch!"* I murmured to myself before retreating back into my thin, brave shell.

"You knew me in the Party as Timothy Horn, but it's Tim Hill — Agent Tim Hill."

If I had any confidence left in my judgment of people, it was crushed at that moment. Agent Waters continued the interrogation, but I couldn't hear a word he was saying. My mind churned over every face I had ever been close to, looking for someone I could still trust. I doubted them all, with the exception of Trish, whose fate I had not yet learned.

"Mr. Logan," Agent Waters said, "Are you listening to me? We know you are a member of the Communist Party."

"Yes…I'm a member of the Communist Party, USA… and a member of the North Carolina Communist P-Party."

"How long have you been a member of these parties?"

"I joined the CPUSA in 1939 and the NCCP a few years later."

"You've been in hiding, and apparently made a decision to come in. You brought some folders with you. What do you want to tell us about the Party?"

I glanced at Tim, then replied, "I've brought with me documents which I'm turning over to you, but you may already have them. Some of the documents were sent from our office in Chapel Hill to offices around the Carolinas, and others were sent to us from headquarters in New York. I picked these because I believe they show the routine, orderly, and professional way of handling our affairs, and illustrates that we are not the bunch of dangerous maniacs people say we are." I opened both folders and then continued, "One of the folders contains a report that we, at the NCCP, were required to send to Headquarters in New York at the end of each year. They are written on official stationery of the NCCP, and they list, among other things, all members of the NCCP, as well as amounts of money we gave to worthy organizations, and unions each year. The second folder contains the annual report of CPUSA listing all members. It is recorded on official stationery. I slid the stack of papers away from me to the center of the table. Agent Waters picked one up and browsed through it. Agent Hill, sitting beside him, looked over the other file. I was surprised at how long they took to digest the lists of members and browse the other papers. The two agents scribbled a few notes to each other and then proceeded to question me.

"Are these names comprehensive?" Asked Agent Hill.

"You mean do they include all members?"

"Yes?"

"I can personally vouch for the NCCP list through 1953. I have to trust the lists that came from Headquarters are accurate."

Tim asked the one question I did not want to answer, "Mr. Logan, I see in the documents you are mentioned a couple of times. We know who you are and your experience with the Party. How much did you tell your father about communist activities, and how much did he tell you about the things he was designing and manufacturing for the war?"

I didn't want to talk about my father and didn't want to answer his question at all, so I simply said, "After I joined the Party, I never saw him again, and I never discussed with him anything about his *mass m-murder* designs." That was not completely true, but it shut out any further questions about my father. I gave them a full report of my fourteen years as a communist and who I worked with.

When they started asking questions about Trish, I said right away that she was very bright, helped us with correspondence, but *never* joined the Party.

Agent Waters brushed away my words with a quiet, firm statement that precluded any response from me, "Don't try to whitewash her, Logan. Evidence in our file, right now, shows she had connections to communist organizations before she came to Chapel Hill. She was very close to her teacher, Elizabeth Ward, who was a communist with ties to the CPUSA. According to our records, Trish joined the CPUSA and the NCCP four years ago, and our information shows she knew more about the communist's activity in this section of the country and had more information about the party workers than almost everybody else. We arrested her two days ago, and she will be interrogated soon." He watched for a response from me, but I didn't give it to him—didn't speak, move, or blink. So, he continued, "Mr. Logan, why does Patricia Basil's name show up on the FBI lists of communists, but not on your lists?"

"I don't have any lists. The ones I turned over to you are official documents from the Party. What's the source of *your* lists?"

"You know we can't tell you that," said Waters.

I glanced over at Tim, who was scanning the names on the FBI document. He then said, "I can tell you this, our lists were given to me by someone in the Party, while I was still undercover."

I fired back, "Then someone has given you false information. Was it Schoberg?"

"I can't answer that question," said Tim in a slow, cool voice.

"Do you have any idea where Mr. Schoberg is now?" asked Agent Waters.

"No, and I don't expect I'll ever find out."

Looking straight at Tim, I said, "*Schoberg* gave you his version of the lists, right?"

Tim's eyes popped up so fast that I knew I struck a nerve. Schoberg never hesitated to falsify whatever documents he needed to accomplish whatever he wanted. I could only imagine what information he manufactured about me and Trish.

"You said Trish was arrested two days ago?" I asked.

"That's right."

"And you said she has not yet been interrogated?"

Agent Waters glanced at Agent Lemay who nodded back.

"It's not our practice to give information about people we've arrested, but since you were so close to her, I will say this. We haven't interrogated her yet because she's in the hospital under guard."

"My God! What did you do to her?"

"I've told you just about all I can, but I will give you one more thing. Before this morning, we had arrested all but two of the communists we were looking for in this region. Those two were you and Schoberg. *So* at 10:45 AM, January 5th, 1954, I'm officially placing you under arrest, and the only person we are now looking for is Schoberg. Would you like to tell us where Mr. Schoberg might be found?"

I pretended to think about it for a minute, then said, "Haven't seen him or heard from him since I left Chapel Hill." I don't know why I lied, certainly not out of loyalty to Francis, but perhaps it was because I wanted everything about him out of my life and out of my memory. If they ever caught him, I didn't want to be forced to testify for or against him.

Agent Hill continued the interrogation with a list of questions from his notepad. Even though I was fully prepared for everything they threw at me, I looked forward to being left alone in a cell somewhere close by. Surrender is always more mental than physical. Agent Waters declared the interrogation over and stood up, which was my cue to stand and be escorted out. Before we got to the door, I turned to Agent Hill and said, "Tim, if that's your name…"

"Yes, the Tim part is right," he said.

"Can you tell me more about Trish?" Tim looked back at Waters who answered, "No, we can't. Her condition is serious enough for us to hold back all information until we know for sure."

"Know for *sure*? What does *that* mean? *Know for sure* she's gonna *live*?"

"We'll let you know as soon as we can," said Waters as they escorted me to a small single cell with a hard bed, a toilet, and a small glass window in the door so I could be observed every thirty minutes.

I sat quietly on the steel bench knowing that all I had to look forward to for years to come would be tiny gray rooms.

# CHAPTER THIRTY-SIX

## TRISH
### FEBRUARY 1954

No one would tell me what my prognosis was. I didn't know how long I had been in the hospital, or how long I had been unconscious. They were no longer giving me any kind of treatment. They were simply maintaining me. Were they waiting for me to die or to get well? Even the FBI stopped its constant watching and started checking on me only once a day.

My nurse was very quiet but very nice. I asked her, "Will someone please tell me what's going on?"

"I really don't know. I'll get the doctor to update you," was all she said. The following day, the doctor came and explained that my condition was currently stable, but they had to wait and see if my body had the strength to reject all the pathogen in the wound."

"Pathogen?" I ask.

"Bacteria from the snake bite, and marsh mud, and God knows what else," he replied.

"What did you mean about my body having enough strength?"

"In addition to the pathogen and the envenomation, which is the snake venom, you were also suffering from

227

malnutrition, that has weakened your immune system, and it's not…it's *not* getting better the way it should."

"You're saying that I could either start getting better, or I could die, right?"

"That's about it. We've done all we can. It's time to be patient, rest, and see what your body is going to do next."

"Then why can't I go somewhere else to do that?"

"As far as *I'm* concerned you can if you have round-the-clock care. If you grow worse, you are to be brought back here, immediately. But for your *legal* status, you'll have to check with the FBI."

The agent assigned to my case had been coming to see me each day at exactly one o'clock, not a minute earlier or a minute later. The next day when he walked through the door at 1:45, I knew something was going to be different. He said, "So you want to go somewhere else?"

"Yes, and I have someone who will take care of me all day long," I answered.

"Where do you want to go?"

"To my farm. But the doctor said leaving here was up to you guys."

"Your legal status with us has changed. You are no longer a suspect requiring constant surveillance. You're now in a category of suspects that we don't have to watch constantly, only regularly."

"How regularly?"

"We'll decide."

"So can I go home?"

"The doctor said he would permit it if you remain bedridden and have round-the-clock care."

I scribbled Linda's name and telephone number on a scrap of paper and gave it to the agent. He agreed to call her. I was sure she would be willing to help me, at least for a while.

"So what's changed?" I asked. "I don't understand why you guys have been watching me for the past few months like I was Al Capone, and now you're only going to check on me *regularly*."

"All I can tell you is, someone has given us information about you. We've checked it out through multiple sources, and your status has downgraded," said the agent.

"Who gave you information about me?"

"Someone we arrested, but I'm not allowed to tell you who. It doesn't matter."

"So what did the doctor say was *his opinion* whether I'm going to recover or *not?*"

"I don't think I'm qualified to tell you about your condition or the doctor's opinion. I'm sure you know that."

"All that's evident to me is that I was bitten in the leg by a snake and it still hurts like hell!"

"As far as I know, nothing is going to change for a while except maybe your location. I wish you well." With that, he left. I was exhausted and faded back into sleep.

•••

"Trishy? Trishy, wake up," a familiar voice said softly. Slowly I opened my eyes to see the tight lips and worried lines on Linda's face melt into a full smile. "Hi, sweetie," she said. "Got your message and I've signed all the hospital forms and all the FBI papers, and two men are going to help me take you to my station wagon. I've got a mattress in the back and you're going to have to lie on it while I take you home. Okay, darling?"

"Okay." I had drifted in and out of consciousness so many times, I wasn't sure if I was half awake or half dreaming.

In the parking lot, two men lifted me from a stretcher onto a mattress and then slid the mattress and me into the back of her wagon. Linda waited until the men left, then climbed into the back to reassure me. "You should be comfortable here. You know it will take a while to get you home," she said.

I touched her arm and said, "What about Lem? Is he okay with this?"

"Sweetie, Lem doesn't know about your comin' home yet."

"Why not?"

"I decided not to tell him. He won't be there when we get home. He had to drive over to Winston Salem today. I'll have you tucked into your bed before he gets back. Allowin' you to come home wasn't a decision I thought he should make right now, so I made it myself."

"O, God!" I cried out.

"It's gonna to be okay. Just wait and see. I'm takin' the rest of this week and all next week off from work, and I'll be with you the whole time." She patted me, moved to the front seat, and we started home.

# CHAPTER THIRTY-SEVEN

## LEM
### FEBRUARY 1954

Halfway down our long drive, Bearcat woofed when he saw a flash of light flicker through the trees from the rear bumper of Linda's car. It was Thursday and I didn't know why she was there a day early. I couldn't imagine what was wrong. Bearcat jumped out and ran into the kitchen ahead of me.

Linda was cooking. "What are you doing here today? Is everything alright?" I said as I stepped from the mudroom into the kitchen.

"Lem, I have to tell you somethin'."

"What's wrong? Is it Trish?"

"They released her today and she was turned over to me."

"What? Why you?"

"'Cause she asked for me."

"But why *you*?"

"Lem, you have to understand she is still very ill."

"*Very ill*? What does that mean? And where is she?"

"She's in bed."

"In *her* bed?"

"Yes, but she's sleepin' and needs to rest, understand?"

"No! I *don't*, and why did you bring her here?"

"We'll have to watch her, while she recovers."

"I was told it was just a copperhead bite. She should be over that by now."

"It was a little more complex than that. She's got to stay quiet for a while. I'm going to take care of her. They gave me a bedpan and I'll be here for a while to help her They said she was sufferin' from malnutrition and her body's immune systems have weakened so much that she's not able to fight off the poisons. It's been a long battle for her. Also, there's tissue damage in her leg from the bite and infection. If she survives this, they can't predict if she'll regain control of her leg..."

"If she survives? Linda, understand this: when she left, I felt like she died. I couldn't bear watching her die again!"

"I don't know what's going to happen. All they would tell me is she's not makin' any progress right now, and that there is nothin' else they can do."

"There's nothin' *you* can do either," I said.

"They said her best medication is good food and rest so her body can get back to fightin' it all off."

"She can't stay *here*!" Linda was as surprised as I was to hear me say that, but I didn't see how Trish could be comfortable here with me, especially if she was struggling to recover. I couldn't say anything else at that point, so I shook my head and went into the living room, closed the kitchen door behind me, and stood in the middle of the room not knowing what to do. Linda continued making cooking noises and Bearcat was happy to stay there with kitchen aromas. I walked to the front window and looked toward the pond. It was past time to let the ducks out, but they would have to wait for a while.

232

I felt compelled to walk toward her room. It was like I didn't have a choice and the floor felt as if it was sloped toward her door. I needed to peek in for just a moment. She was asleep on her back, but her face was turned away from me. I walked to the side of her bed as quietly as a cat. I was surprised how thin she was. She looked thirteen again, but so pale it frightened me. Her long, wavy, brown hair cascaded away from me across the pillow and onto the sheet. In perfect silence, I pulled a chair close beside her. I don't know what I was expecting to see when I walked into her room — a communist? A radical? A hardened face? She looked different, but somehow the same. My kid sister was lying there the way she did each morning years ago. But I couldn't get over the feeling that I no longer knew her. Several minutes went by. She was far too still. I wasn't sure she was breathing. I closed my eyes.

# CHAPTER THIRTY-EIGHT

## TRISH
## FEBRUARY 1954

I opened my eyes. Still half asleep, I had forgotten where I was until I saw Lem sitting beside me. His eyes were shut like he was praying. I felt as if I were fourteen again and still lived at home. I didn't want that feeling to go away, so I closed my eyes and pretended he was coming to wake me like he used to. I hoped he was thinking the same thing. Another five minutes went by before I looked up at him again. Even sitting down, he towered over me. The last couple of months at the hospital I was never sure if I was awake or dreaming, and so without another thought, I heard myself ask in a tiny whisper, "Blunderbore?"

He stood, leaned over me like a great willow bending in a storm, and said, "Broody?" A single tear fell from his eye onto my cheek. He dried my face with the edge of his sleeve and tried not to look embarrassed. His lips trembled slightly as he sat down again and gently held my hand while we silently celebrated a memory...almost lost.

...

Linda came in with soup and biscuits. Lem moved out of the way while she helped me sit up in bed. I pushed with my left foot and left arm. My right leg was still wrapped all the way to my thigh to keep it immobile. With her help, I pushed until I was upright with my back against the headboard. It was impossible not to cry out from the pain, but I held it in the best I could. When we were kids, I remember Lem pulling hornet stingers out of his own arm, and he never cried or let on that he was hurt, but he could never stand for *me* to be in any kind of agony. Seeing my anguish, he instinctively rushed back to the bed, but there was nothing he could to do, and Linda waved him back.

I slept hard that night. I dreamed nothing but awoke early to find Bearcat sitting at the end of my bed watching me as he used to do.

"Come here, sweetie," I said gesturing with my hand. He walked very slowly to my left side, instinctively knowing not to touch my right leg. He leaned close enough for me to pat his head, and scratch behind his ears.

After four days, they moved me each morning to the living room couch. Linda was able to go back to work and return in the late afternoons to cook dinner and take care of me at night. She always had a hot breakfast for me in the mornings before she left for work. Lem stayed with me all day until Linda returned.

During the next two weeks, an FBI Agent stopped by daily around noon. During that time, I never discussed my years with the Party or where I had been hiding. My pain was slowly reducing, but I knew it would take a long time to get over my shame, and put it all behind me.

"I need for you to do something for me, Lem."

"Sure," he said.

"The FBI agent that has been checking on me said he'll be replaced by an agent named Tim Hill. Agent Hill is going to give me a full interrogation right here in the living room. There're a few items and documents I stashed away in my hideout. I need to give them to him."

"I'd love to know where you were hidin'."

"In the Honeycutt Barn."

"What? How long?"

"Since August."

"Dear God! Why didn't you come home?"

"You know why."

Lem sat down and buried his face in his hands, shook his head back and forth, then said, "You want me to get your stuff?"

"Yes, it's in the middle of a little tunnel made of hay, up in the hayloft."

"A little what?"

"A little tunnel made of hay. Oh, also there's a car in the barn that belongs to Will. The keys are in it. You can just drive it back here." He didn't say another thing about it, just went outside, walked around the marsh through the woods to the Honeycutt Barn, and drove the car back twenty minutes later with all my things.

"Trish, I'm glad you're doin' better. But I have to say, I don't know where you are right now…I mean with your past, and in your mind, and everything. If you want to keep that to yourself,…it's okay with me. To be honest, I'm strugglin' with whether or not I really want to know what you did for the last seven years. My bigger problem is I can't picture where it goes from here, and I can't think about the past right now."

"Lem, please be here when Agent Hill interrogates me.

And of course, I'll have to talk about the past."

"Okay, if that's what you want."

I was so glad to hear him say that—glad to know he was on my side again. I didn't know what was going to happen to me, but I knew I was going to need him.

# CHAPTER THIRTY-NINE

## LEM
## MARCH 1954

I was putting feedbags into the barn when I heard a car door slam. A man wearing a suit and hat walked toward the front door. To my surprise, Trish seemed to know him and she let him in. I washed my hands in the mudroom before joining them. "Who are you?" I said.

"I'm Timothy Hill. I'm with the FBI, and I've been assigned to interrogate and monitor Trish," said the agent.

"You two seem to know each other."

Agent Hill looked at Trish, then said, "It's complicated...I met her years ago, and she didn't know I was with the FBI until a minute ago."

Trish looked away for a moment, then said, "He was a member of the Communist Party."

"*What?*" I said.

"I'm still *shocked,*" said Trish, "I can't believe it! I don't think anybody in the party had a clue who he really was." Trish stood by the dining table. With one hand, she grasped the back of a chair, and with the other hand she held a cane I carved for her out of dogwood.

Tim said, "I was a mole."

"A what?" I asked.

"A spy! And apparently the best *liar* I've ever known!" Trish said as she glanced briefly at the agent.

"I was trained to do that, but believe me, it wasn't easy or fun deceiving everybody—especially *you*. I know this is a shock, on top of a lot of trauma, but I hope you're recovering fast. We'll have to work together for a while, and I know it's going to be awkward for you. Let's just call what we're getting ready to do today, *an interview* instead of an *interrogation*."

She shrugged her shoulders and said, "I need to sit down." Her knapsack with all her things from the barn were beside the chair. Tim and I sat on opposite sides of the table, and she sat at one end facing the window. Trish emptied her bag. I could tell by her voice and her blush that she was rattled but holding together well.

"Can I begin?" said Trish.

"Sure, go ahead and begin. You might make my job easier," said Tim.

"I'm turning over to you, letters and documents from the North Carolina Communist Party files," she said.

"Before you start," said Agent Hill, "You'll notice I'll be taking notes of everything that we say and do. That's procedure, so don't let it worry you. Also, you need to tell me how you obtained these documents."

"Francis Schoberg instructed me to compile and maintain the files and keep them safe. That's why I took them with me when I left. All Francis's correspondence going out of the headquarters in Chapel Hill was written by his own hand or dictated to me by phone. I typed them all up, signed them, then sent them out as he directed, and kept the copies I have with me now, and . . ."

"How did you sign them?" asked Tim.

"Tim! Let me finish," she fired back. Tim looked at me and raised both hands slightly off the table as if in a mock surrender. Trish continued, "I was also ordered not to use his name, and to use a name he claimed was his code name, *Lisa B.* He said everyone he corresponded with already knew it as his secret name, his code name, including the people at the national headquarters. From that point on, all mail that I sent out bore that signature, and all mail that came back in response to that correspondence came addressed to Lisa B. But . . ." she looked at Agent Hill and tilted her head forward a little, waiting for him to finish writing and look up at her. "You probably already know about the code name, right?"

"Yes, we know about that."

"I spent about four months hiding in an abandoned barn next door. Nobody, not even Lem, knew where I was. I hid these things there, and now I want to turn them over, but I want to explain what they are first," she said as she placed a large file in front of him. "These are the carbon copies of all the correspondence I typed for Schoberg."

Agent Hill looked over the papers and scribbled a few notes.

She picked up two more folders and handed them to Tim. "These are files of incoming mail; some addressed to Lisa B, and some addressed to NCCP." Trish waited while Hill thumbed through the files. She then picked another folder and said, "This is a file I kept for myself. It's correspondence that was *not* authorized by Schoberg, or Will, or anyone else but Lisa B."

"*You* authorized this mail?"

"Yes, by midsummer, both Francis and Will were slowly disappearing and most of the time couldn't be reached. This stack includes correspondence to and from, headquarters in New York, and other places that I alone made the decisions on how to respond." After Hill eagerly looked through the file, Trish said, "There are some other transactions that I'm giving to you that I need to explain." Hill folded his hands and waited for her to continue.

"I have a letter to me from Francis Schoberg giving me the authority to deposit money, and to pay out expenses from the NCCP bank account using my real name, Patricia Basil. I have a copy of all bank transactions for the last four years."

Trish pulled a pack of papers from the folder and said, "Before you look at the remainder of the documents, I want you to see this one first." She handed it to him. "This is from the bank in Chapel Hill and shows all the last transactions, including withdrawing all NCCP money and closing the accounts. The amount of money I withdrew was $9,443.25 in cash."

Tim read the documents carefully and said, "I'm glad you brought this. We already knew about your closing the accounts and taking all the remaining money. I've been instructed to find out what you did with it."

Trish flipped through a few more pages and said, "Okay, let me show you this receipt from Jane Bonnet at Erwin Mill. The note says she accepted $9,443 in cash to purchase a transportation bus to bring children from neighboring factories to the child-care building at the Mill. Also, at my request, Jane Bonnet wrote on the receipt that after purchasing the bus, the remainder of the money, if any, was to be used to improve the child-care facility. Note the date of the receipt is the last day I was at the bookstore, and the same day I withdrew the money from the bank."

Trish leaned back in her chair while Hill finished reading the documents.

"I personally see nothing wrong with what you've done," he said, "but I'm not a lawyer, and I'm not allowed to give you legal advice. Trish, I have to fill out a rather extensive report of all the things you're giving me, and everything you are saying to me. Other people in the Bureau will determine if it looks like a crime has been committed." He neatly placed all the papers on the table in his briefcase, then said, "I see you have one more file for me. Did you save this one for last?"

"Yes, this last file contains letters addressed to Francis Schoberg that I kept in a locked drawer at the bottom of the file cabinet. I read them many times during the months I was hiding because they mentioned things I never heard about. She opened the folder and placed the letters on the table. She then scanned each one as if she were refreshing her memory.

"Tim… Agent Hill, these items may be old stuff to you, but I would like to know if you, or the FBI, have been aware of them," I said.

"Well, I'm not allowed to tell you very much of what the FBI knows, or knew, but I'll try to answer your questions."

"Were you aware that the Party has been operating an underground assault for many years?"

"I don't know what you mean by the word, *assault*, but I'm aware of the underground operatives they have been training for a long time. We know about the group they call the *backup cadre* who are experienced Party members ready to take over leadership positions in case the existing leaders are all arrested. The *backup cadre* has no written connection to the Party, making them less vulnerable. I'm also aware of a *second* level of workers, further underground called the *Deep Freeze*. These workers have severed most of their ties with friends, and family, and have changed their identity so they are almost impossible to find. It's an invisible network of operatives who can keep the work going on, even if the *Backup Cadre* is removed." Explained Agent Hill.

Trish said, "Okay, I'll skip over to a letter that is by far the most intense and interesting document. As you can see, it was dated June 20, 1953." She paused and looked at him for a moment.

"Is that date supposed to mean something to me?" Hill asked.

"It was written by a close friend of Schoberg, a communist named Jimmy Alexander, on the day after the executions of the Rosenbergs, who, as you know, gave our atomic bomb secrets to Russia. The tone of this letter is desperate. I would guess it's partly because of the effect the Rosenberg's executions had on the already crumbling reputation of the Party, and partly because of this Alexander guy's impatience with the slowness of the Party's *disappearing act,* as he called it. He concludes with a reference to yet *another* underground level, a *third* level, deeper than the others. Did you know about that one?"

"I know almost nothing about it other than rumors. What did he say?"

"This lowest level he said is called *Unavailable Operatives* who will keep functioning in their assigned roles, even if the Communist Party disappears. And he said that there is only one person assigned to provide communication and support to each Unavailable Operative. Nobody else knows who they are. Alexander was assigned to a person who was in the process of making a transition into Unavailable Operative."

"*Good*! Now *please* tell me he revealed the name of that operative," said Hill.

Trish turned the letter toward Hill so he could read the name for himself.

"Oh my God!" Tim closed his eyes, leaned back in his chair, then said, "It was Francis…Of course! That was his plan all along, and everybody, all of us, fell in line with his careful design. Trish, I'm sure by now you realize Schoberg was *using* you."

"Yes, although I didn't really see it until he was gone."

"Well, I'm glad you do now. I know it's painful for you, and as I said, I'm not allowed to give you legal advice, but because I know you, I'll to tell you this: if you go to court—and I think you will—you'll have to prove, as a basic part of your defense, that Schoberg was using you."

"How do I do that?"

"You asked if I knew about the code name Lisa B, and I'm sure you figured out it's your name, *Basil*, spelled backward."

"Yes, I finally did."

"So everything you signed had *your* name instead of *his*, and Schoberg is experienced enough to know not to use a name spelled backward as a code name, but he is also clever enough to know that's exactly what someone who is young and inexperienced, like you, would do—and he knows that's exactly the kind of thing the FBI would expect you to do if you were trying to manufacture a code name for yourself."

"He said he had used that name before," I said.

"He *lied*."

"I just did what I was told to do."

"I know, but the burden will be on you to prove you didn't know the impact of what you were doing. I have to tell you one more thing. Will is going to be tried for violation of the Membership Clause in the Smith Act, so all the prosecutor has to do is prove Will's membership in the Party."

"That's all?"

"Pretty much, but you should know that he took personal care to turn over information that proved you were never a member."

"Why did he do that?"

"Because…I think he loved you and wanted to protect you."

She didn't know what to say, so she just shook her head then asked, "What do you think are my chances?"

"I would guess you're exempt from the *Membership Clause*; however, if you *are* indicted, they will go after you for violation of the *Advocacy Clause*."

"But I never *advocated* anything illegal!"

"The question of advocacy will most likely be determined from the documents and letters you forwarded under your code name to branch offices and workers, especially the ones you said were authorized only by you. If you're taken to court, they'll try to show that you knew about the potential damage to the country as a result of the documents, and they will be presented as directives from *you*, Lisa B to the branches.

"I know the fact that you've turned them over to us, will help your legal position. As I said, your legal status will be determined by others, shortly. I'll get back to you as soon as I find out more. I promise." He placed all her documents carefully in his briefcase, then laid his hand on her shoulder. They looked at each other for a moment, then he left.

•••

Her condition continued to improve slowly, and I walked with her as much as I could each day. She tried to keep me from noticing her pain and never mentioned it.

Tim returned in less than a week. His face was as gray as his suit, and I was afraid of what he was going to say. It was short and simple.

"I've been told that I have to arrest you for violating the Smith Act."

I stepped in front of her and stared down at Tim.

"Lem!" she shouted, "*It's alright*. It's gonna be alright." She tried to pull me back, but I wasn't going to move. She continued, "Lem, he *has* to arrest me. We'll work it out, okay?"

I walked away and looked out the window toward my daddy's grave. I turned back to Tim and said, "Now? Does she have to go right now?"

"I'm afraid so," Tim said softly.

Jack Hemphill

# CHAPTER FORTY

## TRISH
## JUNE 1954

I was arraigned. It was painful, mostly because I didn't understand what they were talking about half the time. They offered me an attorney. Lem was with me, and we both knew we didn't have the money to hire our own lawyer. From the amount I had saved over the previous years at the store and from Lem's savings, we managed to post bail.

My appointed attorney was Sonny Wilson, who couldn't have been more than thirty years old, average height, soft voice, and eyes as big and round as a startled cat.

The prosecutor, Steve Howie, requested a sixty-day delay on the trial date. My attorney agreed.

The trial was held in the federal court in Baltimore, and we were able to meet with my lawyer only once before the trial. Because we had, in his opinion, very little evidence to submit, he recommended that I agree to testify.

Lem drove us to Baltimore, and we left the farm at three each morning. With my cane and Lem's strong arm, I was able to walk all the way from our parking spot behind the courthouse to the defendant's table in the courtroom. My attorney, Mr. Wilson, sat on my left. Tim sat beside Lem on the first row of public seating, and those seats were their permanent places for the entire trial. I frequently looked back at the two men. Lem sometimes nodded and Tim winked or smiled. That helped me through each day especially as things seemed to turn against me.

The prosecutor was a middle-aged, boney man with black eyes far too close together. He spoke slowly and with painfully forced emphasis on his key words. His voice was very deep and clear, and he stretched his vowel sounds so long his deliberations sounded like a requiem. His quirks, however, caused everybody to listen and remember every word.

The Judge was the unmistakable power and authority in the room, and he made certain that everybody knew it the moment he stepped into court. He had a pointed nose which meant he was very particular. His hair was gray around his ears, just enough to make him look experienced and full of wisdom. His temples had a slight pink shadow, which meant he had limited patience.

The prosecutor's strategy was simple. Prove that I was not only involved in a wide range of communist activities, but that I relished them and wallowed in them, and that I consciously advocated dismantling our government.

He called various expert witnesses to review his stack of evidence and explain what each meant to the case. Four of his witnesses were former communists from other states. My attorney told me that the FBI used the same four witnesses for all cases involving communists around the country. His witnesses were paid large amounts of money and were always on call to testify. The prosecutor also brought in Gill Holstrum as a former member of the North

Carolina Party to testify against me. Holstrum spoke as if we had worked side by side for years, even though I never actually worked directly with him. He claimed to know everything about me: my motives, my influence, and my *deep involvement in the Party*. He spoke about my *uncanny* ability to influence people, especially young people, and draw them into Communism.

The prosecutor brought a parade of expert witnesses on federal law, and handwriting. He also produced signed affidavits from several mill employees describing incidents where I participated in stirring up their workers to a point where they staged violent protests against the mill.

My attorney cross-examined each witness trying to find holes in their testimonies, anything that felt thin, or shaky, or doubtful. His failure to discredit most of their testimonies made them seem even more convincing to the jury.

After four days, the prosecutor rested.

Early the next day, my attorney started his defense. He began with Carole and Jackie from the store, as character witnesses. They both said exactly the same things about me and used almost the same words. This exposed the fact that they were not speaking from their *own* experience but had been *coached* on what to say by the defense attorney prior to the trial. Mr. Wilson's strategy was to present a picture of an innocent young woman who was simply a compulsive do-gooder. The next witness to testify for me was Lem. There was nothing memorable about Lem's testimony, except for two unusual questions asked by the Judge. He wanted to know if Lem and I each owned the farm equally.

Lem simply said, "Yes," and then the judge asked

about the size of the farm.

As soon as Lem was dismissed, my attorney announced he would recall Lenny Lansing, who had been an expert witness for the prosecution. Mr. Wilson never mentioned to me he was going to recall that witness. I looked back at Lem who just shrugged his shoulders.

Mr. Wilson started asking questions the moment the witness sat down. He said, "You are an expert witness in Federal Law, particularly the Smith Act. Is that correct?

"Yes."

"Do you agree the law is clear that mere *association* with violators of the Smith Act is *not* considered a violation of the law?"

"That is correct."

"And that there has to be an advocacy or conspiracy to overthrow the government before a violation has been committed. Is that correct?"

"That is correct, but the Act looks at what has been accomplished by the suspect, not just on his motives. What I mean is, if one's behavior causes others to actively engage in things that contribute to the overthrow of the government, then the suspect has broken the law.

"Mr. Lansing, as an expert witness, I'm sure you are expected to be familiar with all the evidence in this case regarding the Smith Act. Is that right?"

"That is correct," said Lansing.

"I call your attention to the Defense Exhibit Number 4." Mr. Wilson picked up a stack of papers from the evidence table and placed it in front of Mr. Lansing and said, "This is a collection of correspondence typed and mailed by the defendant. Have you seen these before?"

"Yes."

"And is this your report concerning Exhibit Number 4," he said as he handed to the witness a stack of papers stapled together.

"Yes, this is my report," said Mr. Lansing.

"The conclusions you wrote in the report make reference to some activities and people that are not in the exhibit. Is that correct."

"Yes, but I had to illustrate how the information contained in the exhibit could be used to inspire subversive activities by people beyond the exhibit."

My attorney placed his hand on Exhibit Number 4 and said. "Would you please identify any page in Exhibit 4 that, *by itself*, could or should be considered subversive? Can you find one, Mr. Lansing."

"I couldn't do that without reading through them again. But the law implies that *any* behavior, even if the behavior takes place over a period of time, resulting in stirring *others* to overthrow of the government, is in violation of the Act. From my experience, I'm *sure* these documents, as a whole, contributed to stirring up the kind of advocacy specifically outlawed in the Act.

"All I'm asking is for you to tell us, from your expert review of the evidence, is there *anything* you found that eventually caused or inspired others to attempt an overthrow the government. Can you show us a single paragraph or even a single sentence that is, in itself, a violation of the law?"

"No."

"I have no other questions of this witness," said Mr. Wilson.

The prosecutor did not cross-examine the witness.

I was my attorney's last witness. I walked slowly to the

stand. My heart was racing, and I tried not to look at the jury or the prosecutor, so as soon as I sat down, I stared at Lem. He gave me a secret smile.

"Miss Basil," said Mr. Wilson, "I want to begin by asking you one very important question: Are you a communist?"

"No," I answered.

"Have you ever been registered as a communist?"

"No, never."

"Have you ever persuaded anyone to become a communist?"

"No."

"What was your job at the bookstore?"

"I checked spelling and grammar, and saw that correspondence was logged and coordinated."

"Did you participate in Party activity that encouraged riots or conflicts that ended in bodily harm?"

"We had a few demonstrations where some fighting broke out, but I don't think the Party encouraged it to happen."

He continued to ask me questions for another five minutes about what I had done at the store. After I answered, he turned the questioning over to the prosecutor.

The prosecutor strutted to a spot in front of me, stared at me for a painful second or two like *that* was the moment he had been waiting for all week. He then said, "Miss Basil, we have hundreds of documents that our experts tell us were written by you, giving instructions to other communists in the Carolinas and beyond. Do you deny writing these documents?"

I replied. "Most of the words in those papers came from other people . . ."

"A little louder please, Miss Basil," said the judge.

I started over, "Most of the words in those papers came from other people. Some were dictated to me and some were written by hand on paper and given to me to be typed. As I already testified, I edited and corrected them all, then sent them out."

"Who signed them?"

"I did as I was instructed to do."

"Whose name?"

"I signed everything with the name Lisa B."

"Why that name?"

"That was the name I was told to use."

"Why?"

"I was told by Francis Schoberg that it was his code name."

"Had you ever seen the name before then?"

"No."

"Do you know that it is your last name spelled backward?"

"I didn't know it then, but I do now."

"How many times did you use that name?"

"I don't know, hundreds."

"Hundreds?"

"Yes."

"And you are asking this court to believe, that you wrote it *hundreds* of times, and never noticed the connection with your own name?"

"Yes, at first I didn't, but I figured it out."

"And you continued to use the name after that?"

"Yes, it's what I was told to do."

"Do you deny distributing documents that came to you from the National Communist Party?"

"We received correspondence from Headquarters in

New York regularly and. . . "

"What's *regularly* mean?"

"Weekly."

"So, it was a lot of correspondence, right?"

"I suppose so."

"And you distributed it?"

"I distributed only as I was directed to do."

"Who gave you the names?"

"Mr. Schoberg and Mr. Logan."

"Did they instruct you where to send each piece of correspondence?"

"I was told to forward everything that came in with directives from New York only to the branch offices, and I forwarded everything that had general information to all names on the list."

"Did you ever send correspondence or documents to anyone, not on the list?"

"Yes, I suppose so."

"Miss Basil, I call your attention to Exhibit 40." He picked up a page from the evidence table. "Exhibit 40 shows a list of books and literature sold in your store that, in part, support overthrowing established governments around the world including this country. They also give detailed information on promoting a fully operating socialist government. Exhibit 40 also includes copies of two newspapers printed by the NCCP –*The Communist Student Bulletin*, designed to keep students informed of the activities of the Party, and *Fighter for Peace*, created to undermine support of our troops fighting in Korea. Did you send these out?"

"I remember a couple of times I was asked to include some old copies of the papers to certain people."

"And are you aware that some of them contained information that could lead to a systematic dismantling of our government?"

"I don't know. That kind of information may have been in a small, *very* small, part of the things I sent out, but I never thought it was relevant."

"You didn't think it *relevant*? "

"I mean I didn't think it pertained to anything we were doing at the time. As I said, they were old copies."

"But you sent them out anyway?"

"Yes."

"Do you deny that you actively advocated and supported measures intended to undermine the efforts of our soldiers in the Korean conflict?"

"I don't know what you mean. Are you talking about the blood drive thing?"

"Yes, at the Negro college in Durham."

"The answer is *no*. I did *not* advocate undermining our soldiers in Korea."

"Miss Basil, I point your attention to our Exhibition Number 37." He walked to his table and brought back a photograph and placed it on the flat rail in front of me. "Is this a picture of you at the college?"

"Yes."

"And what are you doing there?"

"Attending a blood drive sponsored by the Red Cross."

"And would you tell the court what is in your hand?"

"A stack of flyers."

"What did they say?"

"It was a statement that the War discriminated against Negro soldiers, encouraging them not to participate in the blood drive, but I did not distribute the flyers."

"What did you do with them?"

"Gave them back to some of the people in our group."

"Your fellow communists?"

"We were not all communists."

"So you distributed them to communists *and* to noncommunist as well. Is that right?"

"Yes, to other Party workers."

"And what did they do with the flyers?"

"I suppose they handed them out, but I didn't tell them to do it."

"Just what did you think they were going to do with those flyers printed only for that event?"

"I don't remember what I thought at that moment."

"Do you deny that you, in direct defiance of the UNC Administration, helped incite a riot in the streets of Chapel Hill in January 1949 by sponsoring a controversial communist speaker, John Gates, who was widely known to advocate the violent overthrow of our government?"

"I deny I ever incited a riot, and I'm unaware that the speaker that night ever advocated the overthrow of the government."

"Did you know at the time of his speech, he was already on trial for violation of the Smith Act?"

"I'm not sure."

"And did you know then, that under that Act, he was accused of advocating, not just the *overthrow*, but *violent* overthrow, of the government?"

"I can't remember if I knew it at that time or not."

"So, what did you think was the crime for which he was already indicted, and later convicted?"

"I guess just for being a communist."

"Do you deny that when Gates finished and climbed

down from the wall on which he gave his speech, you took his place, and the same crowd that cheered Gates, chanted your name as you raised your hands to them and leaped into their arms?"

"There were others on the wall and I only leaped into my brother's arms to get away."

"Did the crowd chant any other name but *your* name?"

"No."

"Miss Basil, why did you stay with the Party for so long?"

"I wanted to work with a group that was accomplishing things I could never do on the farm. It just made me feel different…different about myself."

"And can you tell the court just what you *think* that you accomplished during those years that you couldn't do on the farm?"

I looked at Lem. I'm sure he was as interested in my answer as anyone in the courtroom.

"I can't say what I accomplished," I replied.

"Why not?"

"Because I don't know."

"Miss Basil, are you aware of the *Jefferson School of Social Science* in New York?"

"Yes."

"What is your connection with the school?"

"I have no real connection. Francis Schoberg was associated with it, and I understand that at one time, he was a student there."

"Do you deny that you delivered packages addressed to that school over a period of two years?"

"I delivered packages to a contact in Raleigh as instructed by Schoberg."

"Did you know those packages involved the school?"

"Yes."

"To what extent were you involved in the content of the packages?"

"A few times Schoberg requested help on wording and spelling for letters that were included with the other documents going to Raleigh."

"What was the nature of the letters you worked on?"

"They dealt with reports of workers I never heard of and requests for other workers trained for things I knew nothing about."

"Did you know that the school was labeled by the Subversive Activities Control Board and by the House Committee on Un-American Activities to be a *seditious* institution?"

"No, I did not know that."

"Did you know that the Jefferson School currently has over four thousand students of all ages, including children, and that they are all taught Marxist-Leninist ideology?"

"I had no way of knowing that. I didn't actually know that much about the school."

"Considering the secrecy surrounding the packages, how could you *not know* that there must have been something extraordinary about that school on Sixth Street in New York City?"

"I suppose I did."

"Then did you know that a branch of that school is a training ground for secret operatives, and these operatives are infiltrating businesses, schools, leadership positions in the federal government, and other important places. And did you know that some of these operatives are disappearing completely underground...including

Schoberg?"

"I didn't know anything about those things."

"Do you know where Mr. Schoberg is."

"No, and I haven't known for a long time."

"Miss Basil, do you agree that you took great pains to hide from the FBI and create clever ways to dodge their surveillance."

"Yes, it was all quite scary and wrapped in secret, and I knew I was being followed."

"So why did you think the Party went to such extremes to protect the secrecy, and why do you think the FBI spent so much time on you?"

"Nobody ever talked to me about what was going on, but I guess it had something to do with the operatives you mentioned."

"Miss Basil, when did you start suspecting that the school was somehow related to subversive activity?"

"I *never* knew what they were doing, so I can't answer the question, but I started to worry a little about it toward the end of my time with the Party."

"So you suspected it was subversive while you were still working with the Party?"

"Yes, I suppose so."

The moment I said that, he stood still and without moving his head, cast his tiny black eyes toward the jury — just long enough for his last question and my answer to sink in, then said, "No further questions your honor."

I looked at the audience. Lem's eyes were fixed on the floor, and his fingers were intertwined into a tight knot between his knees. Tim's face was pale and his eyes were squeezed shut.

The closing arguments for both prosecutor and my

attorney were brief and to the point. Mr. Howie simply restated the law and the evidence, already presented, as proof that I broke the law, and that I knowingly contributed to the efforts of a seditious institute which was working to overthrow the government. My attorney repeated how all of his witnesses swore to my character, and that I had been duped and misused by the Party leadership. He asserted that I was well-meaning, and my only crime was being ignorant of what was going on. He concluded with the statement that the prosecutor had not presented a single piece of evidence that I ever did anything that *directly* contributed to the overthrow of the government.

The jury deliberated for two hours.

Leaning on my cane, I stood beside my attorney while the jury foreman read the verdict. We both looked down. The cuffs of Sonny Wilson's pants trembled.

"The verdict from the jury," the foreman said looking straight at me, "is *guilty.*" Only a slight murmur rose from the audience as if they were anticipating the outcome. I felt myself melting, starting with my feet and legs, and moving upward until my head grew numb and I remembered nothing after that.

The court adjourned and a medic was called. I awoke on the floor of a conference room beside the courtroom. I felt Lem's hand on my face telling me to open my eyes. The medic who was kneeling beside me checked me out and said it was not uncommon for defendants to faint after the verdict is given, but I was okay.

Lem said, "Can you stand?" I didn't answer, but slowly rolled to my stomach, and Lem lifted me to my feet.

It only took three days for the court to decide my punishment. Lem was allowed to stand beside me so I could hold his arm for support while we waited for the sentencing to be read. The judge asked if I understood that I had been found guilty and that he was going to pronounce the court's decision.

I nodded.

The Judge slid a small pair of glasses over his nose and read silently for a moment, then said, "Miss Patricia Basil, this court has found you guilty, and I hereby sentence you to five years in the Lewisburg Federal Penitentiary." I felt Lem's hands tighten around my arm. The judge continued, "But I will suspend the sentence upon the payment of a fine of twenty thousand dollars. You can work out the details with the clerk, but if you fail to pay the fine within three months, you will be taken to the federal penitentiary to begin your five-year sentence. The defendant is free to leave." With the slam of his gavel, the judge left, and the room broke into a blast of disjointed chatter.

I wanted to cry, but I didn't know if I felt like crying for joy over the fact that I didn't have to go to prison, or for sorrow knowing we didn't have the money to pay the fine. Tim gave me a hug. The clerk asked me to sign something, and we walked out of the courthouse to my car. I know Lem felt just as conflicted as I did. We barely talked on the long ride home. Twenty thousand dollars was more than I had ever thought about in my life; however, going to prison was inconceivable.

# CHAPTER FORTY-ONE

## TRISH
### JULY 1954

I sat on the grass and watched the little ducklings paddle behind the big adolescent ducks as they swam in perfect rhythm and obedience to the lead drake. As he paddled around the island, his big white head was held high, his white tail was curled, and his gaze fixed forward as if he were following a vision but oblivious of the fact that they were all continually circling the island, going nowhere. Eventually, I returned to my duties in the duck pens.

...

Lem spent most of the week away from the farm. He asked Quincy to work every day while he and Linda conducted business in Raleigh. He told me not to worry because he might have ways to raise the money. I remember it was a week and one day after the trial. Lem found me in the pen raking straw close to the spot where I was bitten. Bearcat was standing by my side. Lem's face was surprisingly pale for a man that worked outside almost every day of his life. I leaned on my rake as he stroked Bearcat's face before speaking to me. "Linda and I want to show you somethin'", he said in an unnaturally soft voice.

"Okay…Right now?"

"Yes, please."

Lem seldom had surprises and never said *please*. I dropped the rake and followed him to his truck where Linda was waiting. We all three squeezed into the seat together, and Bearcat sat on the floor. We drove to Linda's house. She had three cups on the kitchen table beside carefully placed napkins, spoons, and plates. The room was filled with a fresh coffee aroma. Linda put a plate of cookies in the center of the table. There was an awkward silence while she filled each cup and we took first bites of the cookies. Lem said to me, "As you know, lots of changes are takin' place now."

"Of course," I replied.

"We're all so grateful this prison thing is behind us."

"I hope it is."

"Well, it's time for other changes too." He paused, I waited and sipped more coffee. "The first one is…Linda and I have finally decided to get married."

"Oh, Lem that's *great*!" I exclaimed. I stood and hugged him and Linda.

"When?" I asked.

"Well, pretty soon."

"So you *finally* asked her."

Lem looked at Linda who replied, "No, I finally asked *him*."

"She beat me to it," said Lem.

"I'm just so happy for you both. But you said *changes*. Are there more?"

"Yes," said Lem turning pale again. He continued, "I've found the money to pay your fine."

"Lem! *How*?"

"Trish…I found a buyer for the farm."

I froze for a moment—couldn't believe what I just heard.

"You *can't* do it, Lem," I pleaded. Linda cocked her head slightly and gave me a nod telling me it was true.

Lem bent forward, looked down, and started to speak, but I interrupted. "*No!*" I said, "Why didn't you tell me you were thinking about that?"

He looked at me. His voice was deep and soft like distant thunder. "Because I knew what you would do for my sake. You'd go to prison before you'd let me sell it. You'd give up *years* of your life."

"*Of course, I would!*" Shouting those four words took all my breath, and I had to inhale deeply before talking again. "Yes, it would take a *few* years of my life, but the *farm* is *your* life. Your *whole* life!" His face was stretched into thin, tight lines, telling me he was feeling the same pain that was pounding inside my chest. I realized at that moment what he already knew. There was no turning back. The farm was already gone.

I walked around the table and put my face against his shoulder and my arms around his neck, and I started crying. As his hand clutched my arm, I felt his big head drop toward his chest. He started trembling, silently weeping. His deep heaves shook the table and raddled the spoon in my cup. The farm was lost, and Lem was trying to find a way to live with it, but we both knew that neither of us would ever recover if I was sent to a federal penitentiary.

267

I squeezed Lem's shoulders and said, "What will you do?"

Lem sat back in his chair with his eyes closed until he gained some composure, and said, "Part of my agreement with the buyer is that I get to take fifty ducks with me—forty females and ten young drakes. Linda's got twenty acres here with a pond and an abandoned chicken coop that I can fix up for ducks."

Linda said, "Trish, you're also gonna to move in here with us. I've got this big ol' house and it's mostly empty now. Lem and I can't fill half of it. You can have the whole upstairs for yourself including your own bathroom."

• • •

The next few months flew by so fast I can't remember them. Lem hired some people to move all our furniture. As I left, I didn't give the old farm a long, last look. I couldn't do it, nor could I look in my rear mirror as I drove my car down the drive for the last time.

I never heard from Francis again; however, Tim brought articles to me from various periodicals and pamphlets. All the articles were soaked with progressive and socialist propaganda. Tim wanted to know if I saw Schoberg's hand in any of the articles. Surprisingly, I identified many. Francis had definite idiosyncrasies in his speech and writing style that could only have been written by him.

On the days when Tim came to see me, Lem let him take his place helping me on my daily walk around Linda's pond. I still used the cane and when I got tired, I wrapped my arm around Tim's elbow, and sometimes when the path was steep and rough, he clutched my left arm and pulled me against his shoulder to keep me steady. On warm days, we sat on the far side of the pond with the sun in our faces. On cold days we took a blanket and wrapped it around our backs.

Each time Tim came, he brought more articles and other publications to review for propaganda. After another six months, he found a position for me in the Raleigh FBI office with the title of "clerk", but my duties included scanning mountains of current literature and periodicals looking for communist influences, marking them up, and filing everything that was important. I was afraid that my previous experience with the Communist Party would disqualify me, but he explained that my background made me just the right person for the job. A year later, Tim found an apartment for me in Raleigh, near the office.

At first, I was overwhelmed with the volume of work to be read and analyzed, but I loved what I was doing. I found more articles that bore Francis's quirky style of writing, but more importantly, I was able to identify many statements written by other people, but obviously coached by Francis. The writing used his subtle techniques of carefully planting misleading information designed to guide the public into communist perspectives. I knew that any one of these documents, by itself, would mean very little, and only a few people would even notice its bias, but the relentless volume continued to grow. Within three years, we hired two more full-time clerks to work under me. We assigned identification codes to each document and filed them using the FBI standard system. Our office continually expanded its storage space to archive the material.

Lem and Linda married, and within a year, she gave birth to a beautiful little girl. They named her, *Patricia* after me.

Lem sold both fresh and frozen duck meat at Linda's store. Soon, they added a large, walk-in freezer. The flock expanded to three hundred, which was as large as he ever wanted it to be. By selling directly to the public, he eliminated the middle-man and their new duck farm was more profitable than our old farm had ever been.

After a few years, Tim and I finally married. We had a beautiful boy. Tim wanted to name him *Timothy*, which I agree to, but with the stipulation that his middle name would be Lem.

# CHAPTER FORTY-TWO

## WILL
## FEBRUARY 1956

I served eighteen months of my five-year sentence in the Federal Penitentiary in Lewisburg. It was a bitter, cold day in Pennsylvania when I finally stepped on free ground. The very next day, February 14, 1956, the shining image in my mind of the perfect socialist state was crushed. Khrushchev denounced Stalin's legacy in a speech to the Soviet Congress of the Communist Party. In that historic speech, he launched what has been labeled *the Destalinization of Russia,* revealing Stalin's crimes including the murder of millions, torture of his own people, and mass terror tactics turning the Soviet Union into a police state. Stalin, whose life philosophy embodied perfect communism, the clear promise of socialism, and the man over whose death I wept for days, had been revealed as nothing more than a murderous animal.

Eight months later, Russia invaded Hungry with Soviet troops and tanks, and stomped out the Hungarian resistance, killing thousands, and causing a quarter million Hungarians to flee their own country. The Soviet's grip on Hungary did not simply *reform* the Hungarian government, it *destroyed* it, along with permanent damage to the Hungarian culture.

My excitement about being free from prison was overshadowed by a deep depression and a complete loss of confidence in the communist way of life. By the end of the year, I wrote a formal letter of resignation to the CPUSA in New York and to the NCCP. I was the last registered communist in the region—the last, that is, that could be found. I was beginning to discover, however, that all the things we started during my years with the Party were still growing and becoming too painful for me to think about.

I wrote Trish once a year, and she was good to write back. She didn't mention her work with the FBI, and I could never ask her about it, any more than I could ever tell her how much it meant to me to be so close to her those seven years in Chapel Hill.

Schoberg was never found. No trace of him was detected after he moved out of his apartment. The FBI monitored members of his family in New Jersey for a whole year after he disappeared. They never uncovered a single clue about where he was.

I wanted to believe he was gone forever, but forgetting Schoberg and his long career, was never to be my destiny. My fate would be to watch the effects of my *own* life's work still flowing beside *his*, like underground streams pushing through red clay, and black soil, and secretly soaking the countless seeds we all planted so carefully years ago.

And now, those seeds are sprouting and pushing their heads through the surface. The newborn buds are so tiny they are hardly visible, but so plentiful they silently cover the Earth.

# EPILOGUE

By reading this novel, you have watched the development of the Communist Party in the southeast region of the country from 1946 through 1956. This decade has been called a pivotal period for communism because of its rapid transition from a point of maximum visibility to a place of virtual invisibility; however, at the end of the last chapter in this book Will saw a future where communism no longer needs Russian influence or the support of hidden operatives. His vision warned us of a type of communism/socialism silently evolving and imposing itself on all unsuspecting minds.

By 1958, writings from communist leaders, as well as other sources, were researched and compiled into an accurate list of communist goals. In 1963, the list was introduced into the US *Congressional Record* as a warning of the ongoing, but unseen, communist activity. The list consists of five different categories: International issues, national issues, indoctrination of American youth, introduction of socialism into daily life, and dismantling of American culture including its moral foundation. Today, more than fifty years since they were compiled, most of the forty-five communist goals have been reached. A copy of the text of that congressional document is included as part of this book.

By 1962, national organizations as well as state governments were creating curriculums for the public schools to educate children about the threats of communism. Among others, the list of organizations and institutions supporting this effort include: The National Education Association, The National Congress of Parents and Teachers, the National Bar Association, and departments of public education in various states. A copy of excerpts from the program titled *Suggestions for Teaching about Communism in the Public School* is included as part of this book. The document is currently archived in the UNC Health Sciences Library in Chapel Hill. It was published in 1962 as a call to action because of the urgent need to teach our youth, and all Americans, about the realities and consequences of communism.''

# CONGRESSIONAL RECORD
## Thursday, January 10, 1963

*The 45 Communist Goals,* Presented by Hon. A.S. Herlong, Jr. of Florida, in the US House of Representatives.

The list of Communist Goals was originally compiled in 1958 by an ex-FBI agent, Cleon Skousen. They were taken from the writings of ex-communists and from testimonies in Congressional hearings: below is a slightly shortened version of those 45 communist goals.

1. U.S. acceptance of coexistence as the only alternative to atomic war.

2. U.S. willingness to capitulate in preference to engaging in atomic war.

3. Develop the illusion that total disarmament [by] the United States would be a demonstration of moral strength.

4. Permit free trade between all nations regardless of Communist affiliation and regardless of whether or not items could be used for war.

5. Extension of long-term loans to Russia and Soviet satellites.

6. Provide American aid to all nations regardless of Communist domination.

7. Grant recognition of Red China. Admission of Red China to the U.N.

8. Set up East and West Germany as separate states in spite of

Khrushchev's promise in 1955 to settle the German question by free elections under supervision of the U.N.

9. Prolong the conferences to ban atomic tests because the United States has agreed to suspend tests as long as negotiations are in progress.

10. Allow all Soviet satellites individual representation in the U.N.

11. Promote the U.N. as the only hope for mankind. If its charter is rewritten, demand that it be set up as a one-world government with its own independent armed forces.

12. Resist any attempt to outlaw the Communist Party.

13. Do away with all loyalty oaths.

14. Continue giving Russia access to the U.S. Patent Office.

15. Capture one or both of the political parties in the United States.

16. Use technical decisions of the courts to weaken basic American institutions by claiming their activities violate civil rights.

17. Get control of the schools. Use them as transmission belts for socialism and current Communist propaganda. Soften the curriculum. Get control of teachers' associations. Put the party line in textbooks.

18. Gain control of all student newspapers

19. Use student riots to foment public protests against programs or organizations which are under Communist attack.

20. Infiltrate the press. Get control of book-review assignments, editorial writing, policymaking positions.

21. Gain control of key positions in radio, TV, and motion pictures.

22. Continue discrediting American culture by degrading all forms of artistic expression.

23. Control art critics and directors of art museums. "Our plan is to promote ugliness, repulsive, meaningless art."

24. Eliminate all laws governing obscenity by calling them "censorship" and a violation of free speech and free press.

25. Break down cultural standards of morality by promoting pornography and obscenity in books, magazines, motion pictures, radio, and TV.

26. Present degeneracy and promiscuity as "normal, natural, healthy."

27. Infiltrate the churches and replace revealed religion with "social" religion. Discredit the Bible and emphasize the need for intellectual maturity which does not need a "religious crutch."

28. Eliminate prayer or any phase of religious expression in the schools on the ground that it violates the principle of "separation of church and state."

29. Discredit the American Constitution by calling it inadequate, old-fashioned, out of step with modern needs, a hindrance to cooperation between nations on a worldwide basis.

30. Discredit the American Founding Fathers. Present them as selfish aristocrats who had no concern for the "common man."

31. Belittle all forms of American culture and discourage the teaching of American history on the ground that it was only a minor part of the "big picture." Give more emphasis to Russian history since the Communists took over.

32. Support any socialist movement to give centralized control over any part of the culture--education, social agencies, welfare programs, mental health clinics, etc.

33. Eliminate all laws or procedures which interfere with the operation of the Communist apparatus.

34. Eliminate the House Committee on Un-American Activities.

35. Discredit and eventually dismantle the FBI.

36. Infiltrate and gain control of more unions.

37. Infiltrate and gain control of big business.

38. Transfer some of the powers of arrest from the police to social agencies. Treat all behavioral problems as psychiatric disorders which no one but psychiatrists can understand or treat.

39. Dominate the psychiatric profession and use mental health laws as a means of gaining coercive control over those who oppose Communist goals.

40. Discredit the family as an institution. Encourage promiscuity and easy divorce.

41. Emphasize the need to raise children away from the negative influence of parents. Attribute prejudices, mental blocks and retarding of children to suppressive influence of parents.

42. Create the impression that violence and insurrection are legitimate aspects of the American tradition; that students and special-interest groups should rise up and use united force to solve economic, political or social problems.

43. Overthrow all colonial governments before native populations are ready for self-government.

44. Internationalize the Panama Canal.

45. Repeal the Connally reservation so the United States cannot prevent the World Court from seizing jurisdiction over nations and individuals alike.

## EXCERPTS FROM PUBLICATION:
### *SUGGESTIONS FOR TEACHING ABOUT COMMUNISM IN THE PUBLIC SCHOOLS*

NC Department of Public Instruction
Publication NO. 340, published in **1962**

*Objectives of the Program*

*To create a vital understanding of the belief in individual human worth and dignity in the heritage of Western civilization.*

*To stimulate a greater appreciation of the morality derived from Judeo-Christian tradition, one of the main-springs of Western civilization.*

*To build an academically sound understanding of communism – its history, its ideology, its methods, and its goals. Building a clear understanding of the true facts about communism, against a similarly lucid and true background in the democratic system and tradition, should prove to be the best approach for the preservation of our way of life.*

*To create a learning situation in which the student is imbued with an appreciation for the values that are basic in a free society. In studying about communism, the student will be exploring a way of life that, without qualm or question, employs untruths, half-truths, and the philosophy that "the end justifies the means" in maintaining and furthering its sphere of influence.*

279

*Participants in this rich heritage must be awakened to the fact that their moral and ethical concepts are being threatened by apparently the most powerful amoral force know in the history of man. To prepare the student to read, think, listen, and speak with calm but accurate discrimination in order that he may not fall prey to insidious propaganda.*

*The battle for the minds of youth everywhere, and, first of all, within our own Nation, must be fought with the weapons of the mind. Nor need we fear to use them. The traditional principles of the West, individual liberty and human dignity, are superior in the strength of truth to the false concepts of the communist ideology. These weapons of our intellectual arsenal were forged and tested over centuries of struggle. The plain fact is that we have allowed them to rust unused in the magazine of historical documents; it is time and past time, to draw them forth, resharpen them against the hard stone of present circumstance, and use them in the battlefield of the classroom.*

• • •

### From Chast Carroll, NC State Superintendent of Public Instruction:

*Action on this study should be approached by teachers and administrators with sober and dedicated commitment to their professional, civic, and academic responsibilities. The survival of our national and cultural being may ultimately prove to be dependent upon the depth of this commitment and the promptness with which it is assumed.*

# THE FOLLOWING IS A LIST OF PRIMARY SOURCES USED FOR HISTORICAL BACKGROUND AND ACCURACY IN *SILENT FARM*

*History of the North Carolina Communist Party*

**Author:** Gregory S. Taylor

**Publisher:** University of South Carolina Press, 2009

Based on oral histories, archival sources, and previously unpublished documents of *The Communist International, The History of the North Carolina Communist Party* is the first comprehensive narrative account of the Tar Heel State's Communist Party.

*The Naked Communist*

**Author:** W. Cleon Skousen

**Publisher:** Ensign Publishing Co.; Eighth Edition (1961). Originally published 1958.

W. Cleon Skousen received his Law Degree from Georgetown University in 1940, after which he became a special agent for the FBI and worked closely with J. Edgar Hoover. The *Naked Communist* exposes the fundamental goals of the US Communist Party.

*Cause at Heart A Former Communist Remembers*

**Author**: by Junius Scales and Richard Nickson.

**Publisher**: The University of Georgia Press, Athens and London, 1987

Junius Scales was the leader of the Communist Party for the Southeast region of the United States during the 1950's.


*The Techniques of Communism*

**Author**: Louis Francis Budenz

**Publisher**: Henry Regener Company 1954

Louis Francis Budenz received his law degree from Indianapolis School of Law. In 1935, he joined the Communist Party and became a member of the Communist National Committee and Managing Editor of the Communist paper, *The Daily Worker*. In 1945 He denounced the Communist Party and became a key government witness against the Party. He wrote *The Techniques of Communism* in 1954.


*The Communist Manifesto*

**Author**:  Karl Marx & Frederick Engels

**Publisher**:  International Publishers Co. Inc, 1948, Authorized English Translation

Originally published in London, in 1848.

Silent Farm

Jack Hemphill

www.ingramcontent.com/pod-product-compliance
Lightning Source LLC
Chambersburg PA
CBHW062134170626
46813CB00002B/696